MURDER AND OTHER HAZARDS OF TRAVELING...

Rose sat down, gave a hiccup and a giggle and slipped slowly under the table, a suddenly puzzled look on her face.

Laughing, the men all reached for her. "She's had too much," said Trevor. "I'd better take her back."

Above their heads, a spinning ball of light put their table alternatively in pitch-black darkness and then glaring light. Trevor got hold of Rose and slung her over his shoulder.

He turned to go, one large pink hand firmly on Rose's narrow bony back.

And then he stopped.

He slowly took his hand away and looked at it.

Darkness. Then the ball swung again and they all saw it in the glaring light—the red stain of blood on his hand and the red stain of blood on Rose's back.

AGATHA RAISIN *and the*
TERRIBLE TOURIST

M. C. BEATON

St. Martin's Paperbacks

AGATHA RAISIN AND THE TERRIBLE TOURIST

Copyright © 1997 by M. C. Beaton

For information address St. Martin's Press, 175 Fifth Avenue, New York, NY 10010.

Library of Congress Catalog Card Number: 97-16903

ISBN: 978-1-250-04550-8

St. Martin's Press hardcover edition published October 1997
St. Martin's Paperbacks edition / July 1998

St. Martin's Paperbacks are published by St. Martin's Press, 175 Fifth Avenue, New York, NY 10010.
P1

This book is dedicated
with love and affection to
Jackie and Bilal,
and
Emine and Altay.

AGATHA RAISIN *and the*

TERRIBLE TOURIST

ONE

†

AGATHA Raisin was a bewildered and unhappy woman. Her marriage to her next-door neighbour, James Lacey, had been stopped by the appearance of a husband she had assumed—hopefully—to be dead. But he was very much alive, that was, until he was murdered. Solving the murder had, thought Agatha, brought herself and James close again, but he had departed for north Cyprus, leaving her alone.

Although life in the Cotswold village of Carsely had softened Agatha around the edges, she was still in part the hard-bitten business woman she had been when she had run her own public-relations firm in Mayfair before selling up, taking early retirement and moving to the country. And so she had decided to pursue James.

Cyprus, she knew, was partitioned into two parts, with Turkish Cypriots in the north and Greek Cypriots in the south. James had gone to the north and somewhere, somehow, she would find him and make him love her again.

North Cyprus was where they had been supposed to go

on their honeymoon and, in her less tender moments, Agatha thought it rather hard-hearted and crass of James Lacey to have gone there on his own.

When Mrs. Bloxby, the vicar's wife, called, it was to find Agatha amidst piles of brightly coloured summer clothes.

"Are you taking all those with you?" asked Mrs. Bloxby, pushing a strand of grey hair out of her eyes.

"I don't know how long I will be there," said Agatha. "I'd better take lots."

Mrs. Bloxby looked at her doubtfully. Then she said, "Do you think you are doing the right thing? I mean, men do not like to be pursued."

"How else do you get one?" demanded Agatha angrily. She picked up a swim-suit, one-piece, gold and black, and looked at it critically.

"I have doubts about James Lacey," said Mrs. Bloxby in her gentle voice. "He always struck me as being a cold, rather self-contained man."

"You don't know him," said Agatha defensively, thinking of nights in bed with James, tumultuous nights, but silent nights during which he had not said one word of love. "Anyway, I need a holiday."

"Don't be away too long. You'll miss us all."

"There's not much to miss about Carsely. The Ladies Society, the church fêtes, yawn."

"That's a bit cruel, Agatha. I thought you enjoyed them."

But Agatha felt that a Carsely without James had suddenly become a bleak and empty place, filled from end to end with nervous boredom.

"Where are you flying from?"

"Stansted Airport in Essex."

"How will you get there?"

"I'll drive and leave the car in the long-stay car-park."

"But if you are going to be away for very long, that will cost you a fortune. Let me drive you."

But Agatha shook her head. She wanted to leave Carsely,

sleepy Carsely with its gentle villagers and thatched-roof cottages, behind and everything to do with it.

The doorbell rang. Agatha opened the door and Detective Sergeant Bill Wong walked in and looked around.

"So you're really going?" he remarked.

"Yes, and don't you try to stop me either, Bill."

"I don't think Lacey's worth all this effort, Agatha."

"It's *my* life."

Bill smiled. He was half Chinese and half English, in his mid-twenties, and Agatha's first friend, for before she moved to the Cotswolds she had lived in a hard-bitten and friendless world.

"Go if you must. Can you bring me back a box of Turkish delight for my mother?"

"Sure," said Agatha.

"She says you must come over for dinner when you get back."

Agatha repressed a shudder. Mrs. Wong was a dreadful woman and a lousy cook.

She went into the kitchen to make coffee and cut cake and soon they were all sitting around and gossiping about local matters. Agatha felt her resolve begin to weaken. She had a sudden clear picture of James Lacey's face turning hard and cold when he saw her again, but thrust it out of her mind.

She was going and that was that.

Stansted Airport was a delight to Agatha after her previous experience of the terrible crowds at Heathrow. She found she could not only smoke in the departure lounge but at the gate itself. There were a few British tourists and expatriates. The expatriates were distinguishable from the tourists because they wore those sort of clothes that the breed always wear—the women in print frocks, the men in lightweight suits or blazers, the inevitable cravats—and all had those strangulated sons-and daughters-of-the-Raj voices. Colonial Britain seemed to be alive and well on Turkish Cypriot Airways.

As she sat in the gate, she was surrounded mainly by Turkish voices. Her fellow passengers all seemed to have great piles of hand luggage.

The flight departure was announced. Those in the smoking seats were called first. With a happy sigh Agatha made her way onto the plane. She had burnt her boats behind her. There was no turning back now.

The plane soared above the grey, rainy skies and flat fields of Essex and all the passengers applauded wildly. Why were they applauding? wondered Agatha. Do they know something I don't? Is it unusual for one of their planes to take off at all?

The minute the plane wheels were up, the "No Smoking" sign clicked off and Agatha was soon surrounded by a fog of cigarette smoke. She had a window-seat and next to her was a large Turkish Cypriot woman who smiled at her from time to time. Agatha took out a book and began to read.

Then, just as the plane was starting to descend to Izmir in western Turkey, where she knew they would have to wait for an hour before taking off again, the plane was hit by the most awful turbulence. The hostesses clung on to the trolleys, which lurched dangerously from side to side. Agatha began to pray under her breath. No one else seemed in the slightest fazed. They fastened their seat-belts and chattered amiably away in Turkish. The expats seemed used to it, and the few tourists like Agatha were frightened to let down the British side by showing fear.

Just when she thought the plane would shake itself apart, the lights of Izmir appeared below and soon they landed. Again, everyone applauded, this time Agatha joining in.

"That was scary," said Agatha to the woman next to her.

"It was a bit o' fun, love," said the Turkish Cypriot woman speaking English in the accents of London's East End. "I mean, you'd pay for somethin' like that at Disney World."

After an hour, the plane took off again. Between Turkey and Cyprus they were served with a hard square of bread and goat cheese which looked as if it had been stamped out of a machine, washed down with sour-cherry juice.

Agatha felt the plane beginning to descend again. More turbulence, this time a thunderstorm. The plane lurched and bucked like a wild thing and, looking out of the window, Agatha saw to her dismay that the whole plane appeared to be covered in sheets of blue lightning. Again, the passengers smiled and chatted and smoked.

Agatha could not keep quiet any longer. "He shouldn't try to land in this weather," she said to the woman next to her.

"Oh, they can land in anything, luv. Pilot's Turkish. They're good."

"Ladies and gentles," said a soothing voice. "We are shortly about to land at Erçan Airport."

Again noisy applause on landing. Agatha peered out. It had been raining. She shuffled off the back of the plane onto the staircase, which had not been properly attached to the plane and bobbed and dipped and swayed dangerously.

I'll swim home, thought Agatha.

Having successfully reached the tarmac, she realized the heat was suffocating. It was like moving through warm soup. Wearily she walked into the airport buildings. It looked more like a military airport than a civilian one. It had actually been an RAF airfield up until 1975, and not much had been done to it since then.

She waited in a long line at passport control, a great number of the Turkish Cypriots having British passports. Her friend of the aeroplane said behind her, "Ask them for a form. Don't let them stamp your passport."

"Why?" asked Agatha, swinging around.

"Because if you want to go to Greece, they won't let you in there if you've got one of our stamps on your passport, but they'll give you a form and stamp that and then you can take it out of your passport, luv, and throw it away afterwards."

Agatha thanked her, got her form, filled it in and went to wait for her luggage.

And waited.

"What the hell's going on here?" she demanded angrily.

No one replied, although a few smiled at her cheerfully. They talked, they smoked, they hugged each other.

Agatha Raisin, pushy and domineering, had landed among the most laid-back people in the world.

By the time the luggage arrived and she had arranged her two large suitcases onto a trolley and got through customs, she was soaking with sweat and trembling with fatigue.

She had booked into the Dome Hotel in Kyrenia and had told them by telephone before she left England to have a taxi waiting for her.

At first, as she scanned the crowd of waiting faces at the airport, she thought no one was there to meet her. Then she saw a man holding up a card which said, "Mrs. Rashin."

"Dome Hotel?" asked Agatha without much hope.

"Sure," said the taxi driver. "No problem."

Agatha wondered if there might be some Mrs. Rashin looking for a taxi, but she was too tired to care.

She sank thankfully into the back seat. The black night swirled past her beyond the steamy windows. The taxi swung off a dual carriageway, through some army chicanes and then began to climb up a precipitous mountain road. Jagged mountains stood up against the night sky.

Then the driver said, "Kyrenia," and far below on her right Agatha could see the twinkling lights of a town—and somewhere down there was James Lacey.

The Dome Hotel is a large building on the waterfront of Kyrenia, Turkish name Girne, which has seen better days and has a certain battered colonial grandeur. There is something endearing about The Dome. Agatha checked in and had her bags carried up to her room. She switched on the air-conditioning, bathed and got ready for bed, too tired to unpack her suit-cases.

She stretched out on the bed. But exhausted as she was, sleep would not come. She tossed and turned and then got out of bed again.

She fumbled with the curtains, drew them back, opened the windows and then the shutters.

She walked out onto a small balcony, her anger draining away. The Mediterranean, silvered by moonlight, stretched out before her, calm and peaceful. The air smelt of jasmine and the salt tang of the sea. She leaned her hands on the iron railing at the edge of the balcony and took deep breaths of warm air. The waves of the sea crashed on the rocks below and to her left was a sea-water swimming pool carved out of the rock.

When she returned to her room, she found she was beginning to scratch at painful bites on her neck and arms. Mosquitoes! She found a tube of insect-bite cream in her luggage and applied it generously. Then she lay down on the bed again after having closed the windows and shutters.

She dialled reception.

"Effendim?" said a weary voice on the phone.

"There is a mosquito in my room," snapped Agatha.

"Effendim?"

"Oh, never mind," growled Agatha.

Despite the buzzing of the mosquito and her fear of getting more bites—for if she did meet James and they went swimming she did not want to be covered in unsightly lumps—her eyes began to close.

There was a knock at the door. "Come in," she called.

A hotel servant came in carrying a fly-swuat. His black eyes ranged brightly around the room. Then he swiped hard with the fly-swuat.

"Gone now," he said cheerfully.

Agatha thanked him and tipped him.

7

Her eyes closed again and she plunged into a nightmare where she was trying and trying to get to north Cyprus but the plane had been diverted to Hong Kong.

When she awoke in the morning, gladness flooded her. She was here in Cyprus and somewhere out in that jasmine-scented world was James.

She put on a smart flowered cotton dress and sandals and went downstairs for breakfast. The dining-room over-looked the sea.

There were a number of Israeli tourists, which puzzled Agatha, who knew this to be a Muslim country, and did not know that Turkish Muslims have a great admiration for Judaism. There were also mainland Turkish tourists—that too, she found out later, when she began to be able to tell the difference between Turk and Turkish Cypriot. But the British tourists were immediately recognizable by their clothes, their white sheepish faces, that odd irresolute look of the British abroad.

The air-conditioning was working in the restaurant. Agatha helped herself from an odd buffet selection which included black olives and goat cheese, and then, anxious to begin the hunt, walked out of the hotel.

She let out a whimper as the full force of the heat struck her. British to the core, Agatha just had to complain to someone. She marched back in and up to the reception desk.

"Is it always as hot as this?" she snarled. "I mean, it's September. Summer's over."

"It's the hottest September for fifty years," said the receptionist.

"I can't move in this heat."

He gave an indifferent shrug. Agatha was to find that the receptionist was Turkish and that Turkish hotel servants have had a servility bypass.

"Why don't you go for a sail?" he said. "You'll get one of the boats round at the harbour. Cooler on the water."

"I don't want to waste time," said Agatha. "I'm looking for someone. A Mr. James Lacey. Is he staying here?"

The receptionist checked the records.

"No."

"Then can you give me a list of hotels in north Cyprus?"

"No."

"Why not?"

"We haven't got one."

"Oh, for heaven's sake! Can I hire a car?"

"Next door to the hotel. Atlantic Cars."

Grumbling under her breath, Agatha went out and into a small car-hire office next door to the hotel. Yes, she was as told, she could hire a car and pay with a British bank cheque if she wanted. "We drive on the British side of the road," said the car-hire man in perfect English.

Agatha signed the forms, paid for the car hire, and soon she was behind the wheel of a Renault and edging through the crowded streets of Kyrenia. The other drivers were slow but erratic. No one seemed to bother signalling to the right or the left. She pulled into a parking place on the main street, remembering she had a guide to north Cyprus in her hand-bag, which she had bought in Dillon's bookshop in Oxford before she left. It would surely have a list of hotels. The guidebook, *Northern Cyprus* by John and Margaret Gould-ing, she noticed for the first time, was actually published by The Windrush Press, Moreton-in-Marsh in the Cotswolds. That seemed to her like a lucky sign. Sure enough, the hotels in Kyrenia were listed. She returned to her room at The Dome and called one after the other, but none had heard of James Lacey.

She settled down in the air-conditioning to read about Kyrenia instead. Although it was called Girne by the Turks, most still used its old name. In the same way Nicosia had become Lefkoşa, but was often still called Nicosia. Kyrenia, she read, is a small northern port and tourist centre with a famously pretty harbour dominated by a castle; founded (as Kyrenia) in the tenth century B.C. by Achaeans and renamed Corineum by the Romans. It was later walled against pirates and became a centre for the carob trade but fell largely into ruin in 1631 and by 1814 had become home to only a dozen families. It was revived under the British, who improved the harbour and built the road to Nicosia. Prior to the partition of the island after 1974, when the Turks landed to save their own people from being killed by the Greeks, Kyrenia was a popular retirement town for British expatriates. After 1974 it was settled by refugees from Limassol in the south of the island and once again resumed its role as a genteel resort, with a new harbour to the east of the town.

Agatha put down the guidebook. The mention of the new harbour had reminded her of the receptionist's suggestion of a sail.

She went out again and walked dizzily in the blinding heat round to the harbour, wandering among the basket chairs of the fish restaurants until she saw a board advertising a cruise. It was a yacht called the *Mary Jane*. The skipper saw her studying the board and came along the gangplank and hailed her. He said the cruise cost twenty pounds and included a buffet lunch. They sailed in half an hour and she would have time to go back to the hotel and fetch her swim-suit.

Agatha bought a ticket and said she would be back. She was now too hot to even think of James. The idea of sailing in a sea breeze was too tempting. Let James wait.

Somehow, perhaps because the heat was affecting her brain, she had imagined she would be the only passenger. But there were eight others, and all English.

There were three upper-class ones sporting expensive clothes and loud braying voices, two men and a woman. One man was elderly with a yellowish-white moustache, glasses and a pink scalp where the sun had scorched his bald spot. The other man was tall and thin and sallow and appeared to be married to the woman, who was also tall and thin and sallow but with a deep bosom and a hard air of sexiness about her. They belonged to that stratum which has adopted the very worst manners of the aristocracy and none of the better ones. They shouted at each other rather than spoke and they stared at the other passengers with a sort of "my God" look in their eyes. Their contemptuous gaze focused in particular on a woman named Rose, middle-aged, blonde-haired with black roots, diamond rings on her long, tapering fingers, who was also accompanied by two men, one quite elderly and the other middle-aged. The three were in their way a sort of mirror image of the upper-class ones, Rose having a sexy appeal, the middle-aged man appearing to be her husband, and the elderly one a friend.

Agatha wished she had brought a book or newspaper to barricade herself behind. The skipper made the introductions. The upper-class ones were Olivia Debenham and her husband George and their friend, Harry Tembleton; the lower-class were the afore-mentioned Rose, surname Wilcox, her husband Trevor and their friend Angus King. Trevor had a beer belly and a truculent look, cropped fair hair and thick lips. Angus was an old Scotsman with sagging breasts revealed by his open-necked shirt. Like Rose and Trevor, he appeared to be pretty rich. In fact, thought Agatha, they probably belonged to the new rich class of Essex man and woman, risen to prosperity during the Thatcher years, and they could probably buy and sell the upper-class ones who were gazing at them with such contempt. Then there was a dreary couple who said in whispers that they were Alice and Bert Turpham-Jones, and Olivia sniggered and said in a loud aside that having a double-barrelled name these days was no longer what it had been.

Agatha would have been accepted by Olivia, George and Harry, who were monopolizing the small bar, but she had taken a dislike to them and so allied herself with the less distinguished, who were sitting in the bow.

Rose had a silly laugh and the glottal-stop speech of what has come to be known as Estuary English, but Agatha began to become interested in her. Despite the fact that Rose was probably somewhere in her fifties, she had cultivated a somewhat baby-doll appearance. She pouted, her eyelashes, though false, were good, her breasts revealed by a low frilly sun-dress were excellent, and her long thin legs ending in high-heeled strapped sandals were brown and smooth. She had wrinkles on her neck and round her mouth and eyes, but every movement, every bit of body language seemed to scream out the promise of Good in Bed.

Trevor was besotted with her, and so was the elderly Scotsman, Angus. In conversation it came out that Trevor owned a prosperous plumbing business and that Angus, a recently made friend, was a retired shopkeeper. The quiet couple had taken out books and had started to read and so the conversation went on among Agatha, Rose, Trevor and Angus.

Rose let slip, almost as if by accident, that she was very well-read. After every occasional comment, it seemed to Agatha as if she remembered her role of silly endearing woman and quickly returned to it. Had she settled for money? The diamonds on the many rings on her fingers were real.

The voyage was short but pleasant, the sea breeze refreshing. They anchored in Turtle Beach Cove.

They swam from the boat. Agatha was a good swimmer, but she was out of condition and found that the shore was much farther away than it had looked from the yacht. Relieved to have escaped from the others, she floated on her back in the shallow water and dreamed of meeting James, her eyes closed against the burning sun above. And then she floated against a rock. It was a flat rock and it was a nudge she felt rather than a bump, but she struggled to her feet, suddenly terrified, and looked wildly around. She had not yet got over the fright of being knocked unconscious by someone and nearly buried alive during what she considered as "my last case."

She could hear her heart thumping. She took several deep

breaths and sat down in the green-blue water, which was shallow enough.

The skipper, whose name was Ibraham, was swimming about, making sure none of his passengers drowned or had a heart attack. His wife, who sailed with him, a short, black-haired woman called Ferda, was preparing lunch and the clatter of dishes and glasses floated to Agatha's ears across the water.

Rose's husband, Trevor, was heaving his great bulk, sunburnt now to a nasty salmon-pink, up the ladder at the side of the yacht. He stopped half-way and turned and glared back across the bay.

Agatha looked to see what had caught his attention. Sitting side by side in the water a little away from Agatha were Rose and Olivia's husband, George, giggling about something.

Olivia herself was swimming backwards and forwards with powerful back-arm strokes. Trevor was still half-way up the ladder. The elderly friends of the two women, Harry and Angus, were trying to get back on board the yacht. Harry reached up and tapped Trevor on the back. Trevor turned round and fell back into the water, nearly colliding with the two old men. He began to swim towards his wife. Rose saw him coming and immediately left George and began to swim towards him.

Agatha stayed where she was, enjoying the solitude. She suddenly wished with all her heart that she could forget about James and be free again, free to enjoy a peaceful holiday without being haunted and obsessed by the man. Then she heard herself being hailed from the yacht. Lunch was about to be served. Agatha was reluctant to return. Her brief interest in Rose had fled, leaving her with a feeling of distaste for all her fellow passengers. She swam back and pulled herself up the ladder, conscious of her round stomach. She would need to get herself in shape for James.

Lunch was pleasant: complimentary glasses of wine,

good chicken, crisp salad. Pleased as any tourist might be to find she had not been ripped off, Agatha mellowed enough to join Rose, her husband and friend. She noticed, however, that Olivia's husband, George, kept looking over at Rose from his place at the bar. He said something to his wife in an undertone and she answered loudly, "I don't feel like slumming today."

When the young meet up on an outing abroad, they exchange addresses at the end of it or arrange to meet in the evening. The middle-aged and elderly, by silent consent, simply part with a nod and a smile. Agatha had enjoyed herself on the sail back, for she had told them all about her detective work and entertained them with highly embroidered stories about how clever she had been.

But she, too, after the yacht had slid into Kyrenia Harbour under the shadow of the old castle, simply said goodbye and walked away. Olivia, her husband and friend were all residing at the Dome Hotel. With luck, she would be able to avoid them. She had more important work to do.

She had to find James.

She was reluctant to dine in the hotel that evening, so she checked her guidebook and selected a restaurant called The Grapevine which looked hopeful, and took a taxi the short distance there, not wanting to bother driving. It was a good choice, the restaurant being in the garden of an old Ottoman house. Agatha ordered wine and swordfish kebab and tried not to feel lonely.

The garden was heavy with the scent of jasmine and full of the sound of British voices. It was a great favourite with the British residents, a blonde woman called Carol who served her meal, told her. There were evidently a great number of British residents in north Cyprus: they even had their own village outside Kyrenia called Karaman, complete with houses called things like Cobblers, and a British library, and a pub called The Crow's Nest.

Agatha had brought a paperback with her and was trying to read by candle-light when Carol brought her a note. It said simply, "Come and join us."

She looked across the restaurant. Just taking their seats at a centre table were Rose, husband and friend, and Olivia, husband and friend. They were smiling and waving in her direction.

Intrigued that such an unlikely combination should get together, Agatha picked up her plate and wine and went to join them.

"Isn't this a surprise?" said Rose. "There we was, just walking down the street, when my Trevor, he says, he says to me, 'Isn't that Olivia?' " Agatha noticed Olivia wince. "And Georgie says, 'Come and join us,' so here we all are! Innit *fun!"*

To Agatha's amazement, Olivia seemed to be making an effort to be polite to Rose, Trevor and Angus. It transpired that her husband, George, had recently retired from the Foreign Office, friend Harry Tembleton was a farmer, and that Olivia herself had heard of Agatha, for the Debenhams had a manor-house in Lower Cramber in the Cotswolds.

The wine circulated and Rose grew more animated. It seemed she was a specialist in the double entendre. She had a really filthy laugh, a bar-room laugh, a gin-and-sixty-cigarettes-a-day laugh, which sounded around the restaurant. George crossed his legs under the table and his foot brushed against Rose's leg. He apologized and Rose shrieked with laughter. "Go on," she said, giving him a nudge with one thin, pointed elbow. "I know what you're after!"

Agatha did not think anyone could eat kebab off its skewer in a suggestive manner, but Rose did. Then she, it seemed deliberately, misunderstood the simplest remarks. George said he hoped there wouldn't be another tube strike in London when they got back because he had some business in the City to attend to. "A boob strike," cried Rose gleefully. "Has Olivia stopped your jollies?"

Agatha gave her a bored look and Rose mouthed at her, "Like Lysistrata." So vulgar Rose knew her Greek classics,

15

thought Agatha, who had only recently boned up on them herself. And somehow Rose knew that Agatha had rumbled her act.

What was an intelligent woman doing being tied to the brutish Trevor and a dreary retired shopkeeper like Angus?

Angus was a man of few words and those that he had were delivered in a slow portentous manner. "Scottish education is the finest in the world, yes," he said, apropos of nothing. Things like that.

Olivia had a bright smile pinned on her face as she tried to "draw" everyone out, and did it very well, thought Agatha, although noticing that Olivia could not quite mask that she detested Rose and thought Trevor a boor. She entertained them with a funny story about how the man in the hotel room upstairs had let his bath over-run so that it had seeped down into the ceiling of their room and he refused to admit he was guilty and said they must have let the windows open and let the rain in.

To Agatha's surprise, they all decided to go on an expedition to the Othello Tower in Famagusta the next day and she was urged to join them. They would hire cars. She refused. Tomorrow was James Lacey–hunting day. They had been going to spend their honeymoon at a rented villa outside Kyrenia. She would try to find it.

Trevor insisted on paying the bill, joking that it would be the first time in his life he was a millionaire as he pulled out wads and wads of Turkish lira. Agatha refused a lift, deciding to walk back to the hotel. She was streetwise enough to know that she was safe, and Rose, who had arrived a week before her, had told her with a tinge of regret in her voice that there was no danger of getting your bottom pinched. Rose had also said that there was also no danger of getting your handbag snatched, or of being cheated by shopkeepers. So Agatha strolled down past the town hall and down Kyrenia's main street.

And then she saw James.

He was ahead of her, walking with that achingly familiar long, easy, loping stride of his. She let out a strangled cry and began to run on her high heels. He turned a corner next to a supermarket. She ran ahead, calling his name, but when she, too, turned the corner, he had disappeared. She had once seen the French film, *Les Enfants Du Paradis,* and this felt like the last scene where the hero desperately tries to catch up with his beloved.

A Turkish soldier blocked her way and asked her anxiously in broken English if he could help her.

"My friend. I saw my friend," babbled Agatha, staring up the side street. "Is there a hotel along there?"

"No, that is Little Turkey. Ironmongers, cafés, no hotel. Sorry."

But Agatha ploughed on, peering at deserted shops, stumbling over potholes. Then she saw a light shining out from a laundry called White Rose, Beyaz Gül in Turkish. A man in shirt-sleeves was working at a dry-cleaning machine. Agatha pushed open the door and went in.

"Can I help you?" he asked.

He was a small man with a clever, attractive face.

"You speak English?"

"Yes, I worked in England for some time as a nurse. My wife, Jackie, is English."

"Oh, good. Look, I saw this friend of mine come along here a moment ago, but he's disappeared.

"I don't know where he could have been going. Sit down. I'm called Bilal."

"I'm Agatha."

"Would you like a coffee? I'm working late because it's cooler at night. Trying to get as much done as I can when I can."

Agatha felt suddenly tired, weepy and disappointed.

"No, think I'll go back to the hotel."

"North Cyprus is very small," he said sympathetically. "You're bound to run into your friend sooner or later. Do you know The Grapevine?"

"Yes, I had dinner there this evening."

"You should ask there. All the British end up there sooner or later."

For some reason, Bilal, although probably somewhere in his mid-forties, reminded her of Bill Wong.

"Thanks," she said, getting to her feet again.

"Tell me the name of your friend," said Bilal, "and maybe I can find something out for you."

"James Lacey, retired colonel, fifties, tall with very blue eyes, and black hair going grey."

"Are you at The Dome?"

"Yes."

"Write down your name for me. I've a terrible memory."

Agatha wrote down her name. "A laundry is an odd business for a nurse," she commented.

"I'm used to it now," said Bilal. "At first I made some awful mistakes. They would give me those Turkish wedding dresses covered in sequins and I'd put them in the dry-cleaning machine, but the sequins were made of plastic and they all melted. And then they come down from the mountains with the suit they bought about forty years ago covered in olive oil and wine and expect me to give it back to them looking like new." He gave a comical sigh.

"In any case, can I come back and see you?" asked Agatha.

"Any time. We can have coffee."

Feeling somewhat cheered, she left. She wandered round more streets. Men sat outside cafés playing backgammon, music blared, half-key Turkish music, sad and haunting.

At last she gave up the search and returned to the hotel. She thought she should have gone back to The Grapevine. Maybe tomorrow.

* * *

The next morning she awoke heavy-eyed and sweating profusely. She showered and put on a loose cotton dress and flat sandals. She ate a light breakfast of cheese-filled pastry and then went on impulse into the car-rental office.

"Did you by any chance rent a car to a Mr. Lacey?" she asked.

"Yes, I did," said the man behind the desk. He stood up and shook hands with her. "It's Mrs. Raisin, isn't it? I'm Mehmet Chavush. In fact, Mr. Lacey renewed his rental this morning."

"When?"

"An hour ago."

"Do you know . . . did he say where he was going today?"

"Mr. Lacey said something abut going to Gazimağusa."

Agatha looked blank.

"You probably know it as Famagusta," he said helpfully.

"How do I get there?"

"Drive up past the post office." He led her to a map on the wall. "Here. And then take this road up over the mountains. It will lead you down onto the dual carriageway on the Famagusta Road. You might have come that way from the airport."

"Yes, I think I did."

Agatha set off. Round the roundabout, past the post office, very much an architectural reminder of British colonial days, and so out towards the mountains. The heat was tremendous, but for once she barely noticed it. The air-conditioning in the car was working—just.

The mountains were bare and stark, scorched from the forest fires of the year before. She recognized the army chicanes as she came down from the mountains. A soldier on guard duty beside the road waved to her and gave her the thumbs-up sign and Agatha's heart began to lift with hope. Ahead lay Famagusta and James. And then she thought, I should have asked for the registration number of his car. All the rented cars looked much the same, with red license plates to denote they were rented. And Mehmet probably had a record of James's address.

She carefully observed the speed limit through two villages and then the Famagusta Road, which follows the line where the old railway used to run, stretched straight out in front of her across the Mesaoria Plain, straight as an arrow, and no speed limit.

Agatha put her foot down hard and flew like a bird towards the far horizon.

TWO

†

FAMAGUSTA, called Gazimağusa by the Turks, is the second-largest city in north Cyprus and the main port. It was founded in 300 B.C. by Ptolemy I, one of Alexander's successors, and settled by refugees from Salamis, but remained an obscure village until Richard I offered the area to Guy de Lusignan as a refuge for dispossessed Christians after the fall of Acre in the Holy Land to the Saracens 1291. Under the Lusignans the town grew rapidly, becoming one of the wealthiest cities on earth, with 365 churches, and became a byword for worldliness and luxury until lost to the Genoese in 1372. It was seized by Venice in 1489. The architecture reflects the glories of the Lusignan period, while the fortifications display Venetian engineering at its most impressive. It was taken by the Turks in 1571—Gazimağusa means "unconquered Mağusa"—in an impressive siege from which the city never recovered, and has been referred to as "one of the most remarkable ruins in the world" with its crumbling structures. Further damage to the city was inflicted by the British in the middle of the last century, when they removed vast quantities of stone to build the quays at Port Said and the Suez Canal, and when it was heavily shelled by the Germans in World War II. Famagusta is thought to be the setting of Acts II to V of Shakespeare's *Othello.*

Most of the population live in the suburbs outside the old walls of the city. Agatha was at first dismayed to find out how large and sprawling the place was, but decided to go to the old historic centre, where James Lacey might possibly have been heading to do a bit of sightseeing. She parked the car in a side street outside the city walls and walked on foot to what looked like a main gate. The heat when she left Kyrenia had been bad, but this heat in Famagusta was appalling. She remembered that the English tourists she had met at The Grapevine had said they were going to Othello's Tower. Perhaps James had gone there, too. She asked in various shops for the way to the tower. Most did not speak English, but at last a woman in a small dress shop pointed the way down a long main street. Agatha blundered along dizzily in the heat until she came to a square, and there, wonder of wonders, was a large tourist map. She breathed a sigh of relief until she realized the map was all in Turkish and there was no arrow saying YOU ARE HERE. Cursing, she looked around for a street sign but could not see any. She peered at the map again and finally located the tower. It was by the sea, that much she could make out. She could see some old walls at the end of the street leading out of the square. She ploughed on in that direction. She asked at a café at the corner and was told Othello's Tower was along on the left, and finally she saw it.

She paid for a ticket and entered. A guide was escorting a mixed party of tourists around and had no time for her. He was speaking in English and, by listening in, she learned that the Othello Tower was a moated Lusignan citadel built to protect the harbour and reconstructed by the Venetians in 1492. The name may derive from Cristofero Moro, who was the Venetian Lieutenant Governor from 1505 to 1508—and who apparently returned to Venice without his wife—but Shakespeare's play simply mentions "a seaport in Cyprus" and there is no evidence that it was based on any historical occurrence. The entrance is surmounted by a Venetian lion and an inscription recording the prefecture of Niccolo Foscarini, under whom the remodelling of the citadel began.

Agatha finally left the group and wandered in the shadow of the thirty-foot walls and up steps to the top of the citadel and looked bleakly out at a boring view of the harbour.

She felt she would have been better off to have stayed in Kyrenia and tried to find that villa. She strolled moodily around the top of the walls, feeling the sun beating down on her, feeling sticky and old and unwanted. She looked down the street along which she had come to reach the tower . . . and saw James!

He was heading back towards the square, the one with the stupid map.

She called his name, called desperately, but on he went. She ran down the steps, through the dark archway, and collided with Rose, Olivia, husbands and friends.

"Agatha!" cried Rose, seizing her arm. "Owya? Come an' join us."

"Got to go," yelled Agatha, tearing herself free.

She ran and ran, glad this time she was wearing flat-heeled sandals. But James had gone again. She searched and searched, as she had done the night before and with as little success. She finally sank down in a chair in a café and ordered a mineral water. There was a mirror in front of her. On her better days, Agatha Raisin was quite presentable, having shiny brown hair cut in a smooth bob, small bearlike eyes, a generous mouth, and a trim, if stocky figure ending in good legs. But in the mirror, she saw a tired middle-aged woman with damp hair, a sweaty red face and a crumpled dress. She must pull herself together or James would take one look at this apparition and sheer off.

And then, as she became calmer, she decided she would

wait until it was cooler and ask Mehmet at Atlantic Cars for the address that James had given when he rented the car.

She gave a weary little sigh. So much for her detective abilities. With some difficulty she found her way back to where she had parked her car, and then drove slowly back along the long hot road over the Mesaoria Plain, where no birds sang and nothing seemed to be growing apart from a few stunted olive trees. Dust devils swirled across the road, which shimmered in the intense heat.

Mehmet at Atlantic Cars was cautious about revealing James's address. At last, after more pleading from Agatha, he seemed to decide that as she was a guest at the hotel and British, there should be no harm in giving it to her. James was at the address he had once mentioned to Agatha. She had forgotten it but she remembered it now. It was where they were to have spent their honeymoon. Mehmet led her over to the map again. He said that if she went out on the Nicosia Road past the Onar Village Hotel, which she would see on her right, and took the next road down to the left, the villa would be the fourth one down that road on the left.

Agatha decided to wait until that evening, when she was bathed and refreshed.

She worked hard on her appearance, washing and brushing her hair until it shone, covering her red face with a flattering shade of foundation cream. She put on a simple silk shift of a gold colour, sprayed herself with Yves Saint Laurent's Champagne, and then went out into the dark, still, hot evening, to the car.

Now that she felt she was so close she was almost reluctant to go, to face possible rejection.

She turned off the Nicosia Road and bumped down over potholes, rounded a corner and started counting the villas and parked outside the fourth. It was shielded from the road by a tall hedge of mimosa.

Agatha pushed opened the gate and walked in. She knocked at the door and waited. No reply.

She walked around the side of the house and saw a rented car parked there. He must be home. She walked onto a broad terrace. The large plate-glass windows were uncurtained and a pool of light was spilling out onto the terrace.

She looked in. James was sitting at a rickety table typing on a laptop computer. There was more grey in his hair, she noticed with a pang, and the lines at either side of his mouth seemed deeper.

Almost timidly, she rapped on the glass.

Agatha Raisin and James Lacey stared at each other for a long moment.

Then he rose to his feet and slid back the window.

"Good evening, Agatha," he said. "Come in."

No exclamations of surprise or delight. No welcome.

Agatha looked around. It was a large living-room with an uncarpeted floor. Apart from the table and chair, there were a battered sofa and two armchairs, heavy with tarnished gilt on the woodwork, the kind of furniture called "Loo Kanz" in the Middle East.

"Drink?" he asked. "I don't have any ice. The fridge isn't working."

She followed him into a narrow kitchen. She saw why the fridge wasn't working. There was no plug on it. She opened the fridge door. It was filthy, encrusted with old food.

"Hardly luxury quarters," said Agatha. "Looks like a rip-off."

"It is," said James, pouring two glasses of wine. "My old fixer, Mustafa, used to be on top form. Fix anything for me in the old days—accommodation, furniture, air flights—anything. I paid a month in advance for this place, too. I keep trying to get him on the phone but he's always busy."

"Where is he?"

"He owns some hotel called the Great Eastern in Nicosia. I'm going there tomorrow to ask him what he thinks he's playing at. There aren't even any sheets on the bed, just old curtains."

"How long have you been here?"

"Two weeks."

"I'm surprised you put up with it this long! Not like you."

"I just wanted peace and quiet. Where are you staying?"

"The Dome."

"Nice. I haven't even got a phone. I have to use the phone up at the Onar Village Hotel. I asked the phone company to fix it up but they said they couldn't do that until Mustafa paid the previous bill, and so far he hasn't done that. Perhaps he's ill. He was a great fellow in the old days. Bit of a rogue, but do anything for anyone."

"He's done you, that's for sure," said Agatha sourly. She wanted to talk to him about why he had left without seeing her but she realized he was putting up that old force field of his which repelled any intimate discussions.

"How long are you staying?" he asked.

"I don't know," said Agatha, almost hating him. She took a gulp of her wine.

"Well, if you're doing nothing tomorrow, you may as well come to Nicosia with me and meet Mustafa. Yes, the more I think about it, the more I'm sure he's ill."

Agatha's heart rose. At least he wanted to see her again.

"Have you eaten?" she asked.

"Not yet."

"I'll stand you dinner."

"All right. Where?"

"I don't know the restaurants. I'd like somewhere with authentic Turkish cooking."

"I know a place at Zeytinlik. Called the Ottoman House."

"Where's that?"

"Just outside Kyrenia. You turn off before you get to the Jasmine Court Hotel."

"I'll drive, if you like," said Agatha.

"No, we'll take both cars because you'll be going back to the hotel afterwards."

So much for all my dreams of a hot night of passion, thought Agatha, but still, it's a start.

The Ottoman House Restaurant was in a garden, quiet and serene, candle-light, tinkling fountain. The proprietors, Emine and Altay, gave James a warm welcome. The food was excellent and Agatha amused James with her stories of the terrible tourists on the yacht.

"The thing I can't understand," said Agatha as they worked their way through an enormous meze of little dishes of crushed walnuts, hummus, village bread, pita bread, local sausages, olives and what seemed like a hundred other delicacies, "is why that unlikely sixsome got together. Olivia obviously thinks Rose is beneath her."

He laughed. "I know what you're doing. You're seeing murder already."

"Well, it's odd."

"So how's Carsely anyway?"

"The same as ever. Sleepy and quiet. I've left my cats with Doris Simpson." Doris was Agatha's cleaner. "How's the book going?"

James, Agatha knew, was working on a military history. "Not very well," said James. "I try to start early in the mornings and do some more in the evenings, but it's so hot. It's the humidity, too. Cyprus never used to be so hot. I used to think all those scare stories about global warming were simply . . . well . . . scare stories, but now I'm not so sure. And there's a chronic shortage of water on the island."

He began to talk about Cyprus in his cool, measured voice, and Agatha hungrily studied his face, looking in vain for some sign of affection. Why on earth hadn't she the courage to say something . . . anything? Why couldn't she ask him outright if he would rather she left Cyprus?

At last the meal was over. James insisted on paying.

"I'll never get used to these wads and wads of lira," said Agatha, watching him count out a pile of notes.

"It's cheap for us British because of the exchange rate," said James, "but not much fun for the locals."

They walked out to their cars. Agatha put her face up to be kissed and he pecked her on the cheek. Despite the heat of the evening, his lips were cool and passionless. Not even a frisson, thought Agatha miserably.

"What time tomorrow?" she asked.

"I'll call for you at ten o'clock."

Agatha got into the car and drove back to her hotel. There was a wedding reception taking place in the hotel lounge: music, dancing, bride and groom, mothers, fathers, assorted relatives. The bride was very beautiful and her face shone with happiness. Agatha stood in the doorway, watching. She felt a wave of self-pity engulfing her. There had been no white wedding for Agatha Raisin, just a brief ceremony in a registry office in London when Jimmy Raisin had married her. Now, there never would be. She was too old to go to any altar in white. A plump little Turkish woman saw her standing there and smiled and beckoned her into the room, but Agatha shook her head sadly and walked away.

There was the outing with James to look forward to, but right at that moment she could not. His coldness, his matter-of-fact coldness, had quenched all her rosy dreams. Her pursuit of him to this island now seemed pushy and vulgar.

She went into her room and opened up the windows and shutters and stepped out onto the balcony. Out over the sea in the direction of Turkey, a long flash of lightning stabbed down over the heaving sea, and thunder rumbled. A damp fresh breeze struck her cheek. She leaned on the railing of the balcony and watched the approach of the storm, standing there until the first large warm raindrops struck her cheek before retreating into her room. All night long the thunder crashed and rolled as she tossed and turned in bed. But at least, she thought, before she finally fell into a last fitful bout of sleep, the morning would probably be clear and fresh and that would raise her spirits.

* * *

But the morning was grey and damp and sticky, with lowering clouds lying over a stormy sea. She ate her breakfast, looking cautiously around from time to time in case Olivia, husband and friend came in, but there was no sign of them.

James called for her promptly at ten o'clock. He was wearing a short-sleeved blue cotton shirt which matched his eyes, eyes which surveyed Agatha, neat in tailored white blouse and linen skirt, with a guarded look.

They drove out along the road over the mountains to Nicosia. "There is a story that the Saudis paid for this to be a dual carriageway," said James, breaking a long silence. "When a Saudi official came to open the dual carriageway and he only saw this two-lane highway, he was outraged. 'Where's the other half?' he kept demanding."

"And what had happened to the other half?" asked Agatha.

"Probably went straight into someone's pocket and ended up as a high-rise or a hotel."

They crested a hill and there, down on the plain, lay Nicosia, Lefkoşa to the Turks, bathed in a yellow gleam of sunlight which pierced the low, threatening clouds.

"It looks like one of the Cities of the Plain," said Agatha.

He turned slightly and looked at her in surprise.

"Oh, yes, I do have an imagination, James," said Agatha. "It often leads me into making silly mistakes."

Like this trip to Cyprus, thought Agatha silently.

Aloud she asked, "Where is the Great Eastern Hotel?"

"Just on the road into Nicosia, on the left. I'm sure I'll find old Mustafa has been ill."

"When did you last see him?"

"Oh, about 1970."

"Didn't he come around to see you settled in?"

"No," said James. "I arranged everything by phone. He said he would leave the key with a neighbour. I can't under-

29

stand it. I've rented places from Mustafa in the old days and they were always all right."

"People change," said Agatha on a sigh. The greyness and heaviness of the day was getting to her. Nor was she impressed with the outskirts of Nicosia, which looked just like any dreary London suburb.

"Here we are," said James. "I'll need to circle around." He parked outside a large modern hotel, or rather, the hotel was of modern architecture, but it already seemed to be falling into decay. The front doors were firmly locked.

"I must find out what's happened to Mustafa," said James. "Let's try round the back. Maybe there's some life in the kitchens."

They picked their way up a cracked path at the side of the hotel and suddenly were confronted with a large, heavy-set man with beetling brows and flat, dead eyes.

He asked them something in Turkish.

James shook his head and said, "We're English. Where's Mustafa?"

He jerked his head to indicate they should follow him into a side door of the hotel.

"A goon looks like a goon no matter what nationality," muttered James. "I don't like the look of this."

The man led them along a dark passage. Water dripped down through the ceilings and made puddles on the uncarpeted passageway. Must be an extension, thought Agatha. The rain can't possibly have dripped its way down through all the hotel floors.

The suddenly found themselves in a dark bar. There were a few Turkish soldiers sitting around and plenty of James's goons, and girls, girls, girls. Their guide pointed to two chairs. They sat down.

"Is this a brothel?" asked Agatha.

"Yes," said James curtly.

"Are those Turkish girls?"

"No, they call them Natashas. They come from the old Soviet Bloc countries—Hungary, Romania, places like that."

A slim man with a triangular face approached them and said in perfect English, "Can I help you?"

He was wearing a well-tailored suit and his eyes were bright and merry. He looked like a picture of harlequin without the white paint and he was somehow more frightening than the goons. Agatha decided in that moment that intelligent evil was more frightening than anything else and she was sure this harlequin was evil.

"I am James Lacey. I rented a house from Mustafa and it is in a disgraceful condition. Where is he?"

"Mustafa is in London."

"And when will he return?"

The man spread his hands and shrugged his well-tailored shoulders.

Then he said, "If you leave your phone number, I will get him to call you when he comes back."

"I don't have a phone," said James crossly. "In fact, that is one of my many complaints. Does Mustafa own this place?"

"Yes."

James's lip curled with distaste. "Then he is no longer the Mustafa I knew."

"If I may show you out . . ." said the man politely. His eyes looked amused, amused at their outrage.

"Probably drugs as well as being a Natasha pasha," said James as they got back into his rented car.

"What's a Natasha pasha?"

"Brothel-keeper."

"I don't know what took you so long to complain," said Agatha. "Let's find the tourist office and put in a complaint."

"It wouldn't do us any good. I think I should cut my losses and find somewhere else. The manager at the Onar Village Hotel, Stefan, has been letting me use the telephone and fax. I'll call there and see if he knows of any place I can move to."

31

At James's suggestion, before they went back, they went into the old part of Nicosia, wandered around the covered market, Agatha being restrained by James from haggling for a brass pepper mill. Unlike mainland Turkey, you were expected to pay the marked price. Then they went to the Saray Hotel for lunch. The centre of Nicosia was a pleasant, friendly place with a lot of interesting old buildings and shops. Agatha would have been happy to spend the day there, exploring, but James was determined to set out back to the Onar Village Hotel and see if he could find somewhere else to live.

"Why not just return with me to Carsely?" asked Agatha as he drove out of Nicosia.

"I'm not yet ready for that," he said and then drove on in silence.

At the Onar Village Hotel, the manager, Stefan, told them that the hotel housekeeper was leaving for Australia and would perhaps rent them her home. It was out at Alsancak, next to the Altinkaya fish restaurant.

They drove there to meet the housekeeper and her friendly family. It was a large villa near the beach and seemed to have every home comfort. To Agatha's dismay, she heard James say he would take it for three months, perhaps longer.

The door opened and Bilal of the laundry came in with his English wife. "These are my friends," said the housekeeper. "They will look after you."

Bilal smiled. "So you found Mr. Lacey," he said to Agatha.

James looked sharply at Agatha. "We've met before," muttered Agatha, who somehow had no wish to tell James how she had run after him.

James agreed to move in the following day.

"What about Mrs. Raisin?" asked Bilal, his eyes bright and mischievous. "Loads of room here. No need to go on paying a hotel bill."

Jackie, Bilal's wife, a woman in her forties with intelligent eyes and a rosy tan that Agatha envied, said, "Yes, why don't you move in as well, Mrs. Raisin?"

"I suppose so," said James grudgingly. "Mrs. Raisin is only here on a short holiday."

Agatha knew in that moment that if she said, yes, she would stay, James would hate it, would think she was crowding him.

"Thank you," she said brightly. "I'll check out of the hotel tomorrow."

James gave a little sigh but settled down to arrange the rent and ask about local shops.

Agatha went upstairs. There was a big bedroom with a double bed. French windows opened up onto an upstairs terrace. Next to it was a single bedroom. Then, through a narrow bathroom and down wooden steps, there was another bedroom with a view of the sea and with a single bed under the window.

She would take this, she decided, and give James the double bedroom.

She went back downstairs by a back stair which led off her new room. There was a summer living-room which looked out onto a terrace and garden, and a winter living-room where the negotiations were taking place. The kitchen was vast. Looking out of the kitchen window, she saw the car-park of the restaurant through a screen of mimosa bushes.

Jackie joined her. "That's a very good fish restaurant. The manager, Umit Erener, is a friend of ours."

"I might try it."

Jackie's eyes twinkled. "Does Mr. Lacey always call you Mrs. Raisin?"

"Only in the company of strangers," said Agatha stiffly. All the time she was thinking, I shouldn't have said I would stay. I'll have driven him further into his shell. "He's old-fashioned."

As she and James finally drove off. Agatha said, "I've

33

selected that little single bedroom at the front of the house, you know, the one you have to walk through the bathroom to get to."

He swivelled his head angrily and glared at her. "You WHAT?"

"I—I said I thought I'd sleep in that little room at the front of—"

"I thought that's what you said, Agatha, but I can hardly believe my ears. I am renting this villa, not you, and yet you immediately take over and decide where *you* want to sleep!"

"I'm sorry," said Agatha huffily. "I thought you would like the master bedroom."

"Just stop thinking for me, will you?"

Agatha bit her lip. She had been about to say, forget it, she would stay at the hotel, but the whole reason she was there was to get him back.

Why do you want such a cold pig? sneered a voice in her head.

When he stopped outside The Dome, he said in a cold voice and staring straight ahead, "No doubt I shall see you to-morrow."

Agatha cracked. "Oh, stuff you and your stupid villa," she howled, tears starting to her eyes.

"I'm sorry," he said quickly. "I'm still angry at being ripped off by Mustafa and I shouldn't have taken it out on you. See here, we'll have dinner tonight. I'll see you in the dining-room of your hotel at eight."

Agatha gave a watery sniff. "See you then."

The trouble was, she thought, when she stood out on her hotel balcony and watched the surge of the grey-black Mediterranean pounding on the rocks below, that being in a foreign country made her feel lost and vulnerable.

But they would have dinner together. In the evening, the tables were set out in the open air on the terrace. She would re-serve a table at the edge overlooking the sea. She would put on her best gown.

She walked back in and studied her face in the glass. Oh, those treacherous lines around the eyes and round the mouth! She slapped on a face pack and settled down to wait for the evening ahead.

By five to eight, she was ready to go downstairs to the dining-room. She felt she had never looked better. Her hair was brushed and shining, her face smooth under carefully applied foundation, lipstick and mascara. She was wearing a low-cut red chiffon gown and high-heeled black patent-leather shoes. She felt sure she had lost inches already with the sauna-like heat.

Her mind wandered off into a dream. The blustery wind had stopped blowing. They would sit at that table she had reserved earlier, looking at each other across the candle-light. At the end of the meal, he would reach across the table and take her hand. An electric current would pass between them. Silently he would lead her up to her room and then . . . and then . . .

She jerked out of her dream with an effort. It was now eight o'clock and James was always punctual.

When she stood at the entrance to the dining-room, the noise hit her full in the face. It was Saturday night and a belly-dancer was performing. Everyone was clapping her and cheering and laughing.

And then she saw James. He was not sitting at the table she had reserved for them but at a table in the centre of the dining-room—with Rose, Olivia, Harry, George, Angus and Trevor. They waved to her and she went reluctantly to join them.

"We heard your fellah asking the metter dee for Mrs. Raisin's table," shouted Rose, "so we says, she's a friend of ours. Come and join the party. Park your bum next to Trevor and we'll have some wine."

Agatha looked desperately at James but he was talking to Olivia. She tried to talk to Trevor, but the noise of the music was so loud that she gave up. How was Olivia managing to cope? Probably braying as usual.

The belly-dancer approached their table and Trevor asked her to dance on it for them, which she promptly did. But she was joined by Rose, who climbed up on the table as well and began gyrating beside the belly-dancer. Agatha closed her eyes to block out the sight, for Rose was wearing a very short, fringed skirt and no knickers.

At last, with a roll of drums, the belly-dancer swayed out of the restaurant and the music fell silent.

"That was a bit of all right, hey, James," said Rose, batting her eyelashes at him.

"Not enough belly," said James. "Too thin."

"That's why you like old Aggie," shrieked Rose. "Good armful."

Agatha's glass of wine trembled in her hand. She was restraining herself from throwing the contents into Rose's face.

James began talking to Olivia and George. It seemed they had friends in common, which left Agatha to talk to the common friends, namely Rose, Trevor and Angus.

"So what've you bin doing today, Agatha?" asked Rose.

"We went to rent a villa together," said Agatha stiffly.

"Fast worker, Aggie," said Rose.

"She isn't the only one," said Trevor, his voice thick with drink.

"I wasn't talking about Agatha. I was talking about James," said Rose. "How did you meet him, Agatha?"

"We solved several murder cases together," said Agatha. "He's my neighbour."

Rose's eyes sharpened. "After we 'ad that talk on the boat, I remembered something. It came back to me. You pair were about to get married when your husband turned up at the wedding. Read it in the papers and laughed myself silly. You're a character, Agatha."

"And I wonder a lot about people," said Agatha in a thin

36

voice. "I often wonder, for example, why some clever women insist of behaving like stupid sluts."

There was a silence. James had paused in his conversation with Olivia and heard Agatha's remark. So had Olivia, and her eyebrows had risen to her hairline.

And then Trevor said, "I've often noticed the same thing. That's why I'm lucky I've got Rose. She's always just herself."

"Yes," said Angus portentously, "with Rose, what you see is what you get."

Rose winked at Agatha, who immediately felt ashamed of herself. "Let's have another couple of bottles of wine on me," she said.

This was hailed with cheers and only then did Agatha regret her generosity. With the exception of James, the party began to get drunk. They had already drunk a copious amount, and Agatha's gift tipped them over the edge.

Agatha began to wonder if she could manage to persuade James to go somewhere after the meal for a quiet coffee, somewhere quiet. There was a pleasant outdoor café along from the hotel. They would sit there and chat. They would . . .

"The night is young," cried Rose, her face flushed and her eyes glittering. "There's disco along the coast. Let's boogie."

Agatha pleaded with her eyes at James, but he made no move to protest. She opened her mouth to say she was tired, she wanted to go to bed. But Olivia smiled at James and said, "Good idea. First dance with me, James."

Agatha tightened her lips. Olivia was wearing a jade-green silk shift and a jade necklace. She kept bending forward every time she spoke to James, letting the cleavage of her dress droop. He must be able to see her navel, thought Agatha.

Worse happened outside the hotel. James went off with Olivia, George and Harry in one car, leaving Agatha to follow with Rose, Trevor and Angus.

They stopped at a disco attached to a hotel outside Karaoğlanoğlu, a place which looked like a frontier town, just along the coast from Kyrenia. More noise, more thudding music. Agatha's head ached.

James took the floor with Olivia and started throwing himself energetically about in movements which seemed to have nothing to do with the beat of the music.

Angus asked Agatha for a dance, put a beefy hand at her waist and tried to propel her in a foxtrot to the disco beat. "I think we should sit down," shouted Agatha in his ear after he had trodden on her feet, painfully, for about the third time.

"Aye, I'm no' verra good at this," said Angus. "You should see me do an eightsome reel."

"Really?" said Agatha politely.

They sat down at a table at the edge of the floor. Gradually the others joined them. Rose sat down, gave a hiccup and a giggle and slipped slowly under the table, a suddenly puzzled look on her face.

Laughing, the men all reached for her. "She's had too much," said Trevor. "I'd better take her back."

"Which hotel are you in?" asked James.

"The Celebrity, along at Lapta."

Above their heads, a spinning ball of light put their table alternatively in pitch-black darkness and then glaring light. Trevor got hold of Rose and slung her over his shoulder. "Better take baby home," he said with a grin.

He turned to go, one large pink hand firmly on Rose's narrow bony back.

And then he stopped.

He slowly took his hand away and looked at it.

Darkness. Then the ball swung again and they all saw it in the glaring light—the red stain of blood on his hand and the red stain of blood on Rose's back.

THREE

†

THE police did not allow anyone to leave the disco until the following morning. The duty officer from the British High Commission was there to look after his compatriots. They were questioned over and over again. Agatha could only shake her head each time and say she did not know what could have possibly happened. Rose, she said, appeared to have become the worse for drink and had sunk under the table. The men had crowded around, laughing, to reach down to get her, but there were a lot of men other than those in their own party there when Rose was pulled out from under the table.

The police force in north Cyprus is still run on British lines. They keep a considerably lower profile than the army, who have their own police force, the ASIZ. The civil police work is in close conjunction with the tourist department, and visitors are usually treated with a special tolerance and help-fulness. The crime rate is exceptionally low, and the civil police are used to dealing mostly with traffic accidents.

But here was the murder of a British tourist. And the

authorities were determined to solve it. Detective Inspector Nyall Pamir, who spoke good English, during one of his many interrogations of Agatha seemed to think it was a crime of passion. Agatha asked why. Pamir said that Rose was knickerless and that seemed to him to be as good a clue as any. He was a short, tubby man with skin as dark as an Indian's and small black eyes which gave nothing away. Agatha had an odd feeling he was trying to be funny but then decided she must be wrong.

Rose had been stabbed with a thin, sharp instrument, probably some sort of knife, was the preliminary finding.

They were all told not to leave the island, and to hold themselves ready for further questioning. Then they all shuffled out into the blazing sunlight of early morning.

Angus stood there, old and trembling, tears rolling down his cheeks. "Rose, gone," he kept saying. "I cannae believe it." Trevor was grim and silent.

To Agatha's relief, because she wanted time to rest and think, James had ordered a taxi for both of them. He dropped her at her hotel, saying, "I'll see you at the villa in an hour. We'll talk then."

Agatha packed slowly and carefully. She found she was reluctant to check out. There was something safe about The Dome with its balconied rooms and large ornate lounges. And she hadn't even had a swim yet at that pool. She was too tired to think much about who had murdered Rose or why.

She was finally finished. She took a last look round and then went down to the reception and paid her bill. This time there was a Turkish Cypriot girl on duty at the desk. News travels fast in north Cyprus, and so it transpired that the girl had not only heard of the murder but that Agatha had been present at the disco.

"How bad for you," she said sympathetically as Agatha paid her bill. "It was probably one of those mainland Turks. They're not like us. Always getting drunk and stabbing people."

This was a wild exaggeration and Agatha did not yet

know that the Turkish Cypriots regard themselves as being superior to the mainland Turks, and she found it comforting. At first the thought had crossed her mind that if she and James entered into another murder hunt, it might be the very thing to draw them back together again, but now she had a weary distaste for the whole business and a longing for home. She searched around her mind for that old obsession for James, but it seemed to have died.

Soon she set out in her rented car along the road out of Kyrenia, past the disco where police cars were still lined up, carefully observing the thirty-miles-an-hour speed limit, out past the monument to the Turkish landings, and then turned right by a sign to Sunset Beach and parked beside the hedge of cactus and mimosa behind James's car.

The front door was standing open. She lugged her cases inside. She called, "James!" but there was no sound but the wind and the sea. She walked through the kitchen out into the garden. James was sitting in a garden chair under an orange tree, intently listening to the news on the BBC World Service.

"Anything?" asked Agatha.

He shook his head. "You wouldn't think it was the *British* Broadcasting Service," he complained. "I can tell you everything that's going on in Africa and Russia, but not a word about anyone or anything British."

Agatha pulled up a little white wrought-iron garden chair and sat down opposite him. Behind the orange tree was a vine, its leaves rustling in the breeze. The air was heavy with the scent of vanilla from a large plant to Agatha's left. Her eyes felt gritty with fatigue.

"I hope you had a shower before you left the hotel," said James.

"I haven't even changed my clothes," said Agatha, indicating her party dress. "Why?"

"This isn't a day for water. There might be some later. I think we both need sleep."

41

"Which bedroom is mine?"

"The one you chose. I'll take your luggage up."

They went inside. He carried up her cases to her new room. With a curt little nod, he left her. Agatha stripped off her clothes and fell naked on top of the bed. The windows were open and a light breeze was blowing in, bringing with it snatches of voices from the beach. She plunged down immediately into a heavy sleep and awoke three hours later, sweating from every pore. The breeze had died and the stifling humidity had returned.

Still naked, she trekked up the shallow wooden steps and through to the bathroom. The bathroom had a door at either end. The one opposite to the one she had entered suddenly opened and James came in.

"There's water now," he said, looking at her. "You can have a shower and then come downstairs. I've got some cold meat and salad."

When he had shut the door Agatha looked crossly down at her body. Well, although her breasts did not yet sag and she was not cursed with cellulite, she supposed it was not a body to drive a man to passion. Besides, James had seen all of it before.

After she had showered and changed into shorts and a cotton shirt and flat-heeled sandals, she felt better. She went downstairs. James had set out a meal for both of them on the kitchen table. Agatha suddenly realized she was ravenous and had not eaten since the night before.

"What are we going to do about this murder, Agatha?" asked James.

"The receptionist at the hotel said it was probably some mainland Turk."

"They get blamed for a lot, but believe me, they don't go around murdering British tourists."

"The thing that gets me," said Agatha, "is that if, say, she was murdered on the dance floor, wouldn't she have screamed or cried out?"

"Not necessarily. It was some sort of very thin blade, remember."

"Could someone have stabbed her while everyone was trying to drag her out from under the table?"

"She was lying on her back," said James. "I'm sure she was. Yes, she was on her back when Trevor slid her out from under the table. If that's the case, there'll have been smears of blood on the floor."

"I think the clue to the whole thing," said Agatha eagerly, "is in the odd friendship between Olivia and her lot and Rose and her lot."

"Tell me again how you met them."

So Agatha told him of the sail on the yacht, how Olivia, George and Harry had hogged the small bar and had been contemptuous of the rest. Then how, when she had been swimming, she had seen Rose and George laughing together until Trevor saw them. She moved on to the scene in The Grapevine and how, underneath Rose's screeching vulgarity, there was a well-read, intelligent, shrewd mind.

When she had finished, they heard a knock at the door. "That'll be the police," said James, getting to his feet. "I think we should have a crack at finding out who did this ourselves, Agatha, so keep your speculations to yourself." He went off before she could reply.

He returned with Detective Inspector Nyall Pamir. He sat down at the table and surveyed Agatha with those little black eyes of his which gave nothing away.

"Aren't your colleagues going to join you?" asked James.

"They can wait outside," said Pamir. "This is an informal chat. I would like you both to report to the police headquarters in Lefkoşa tomorrow at ten in the morning for an official interrogation."

He folded his small fat hairy hands on the table in front of him. They looked like two small furry animals.

"Now, Mrs. Raisin," he began, "who do you think murdered Rose Wilcox?"

43

Agatha glanced at James, who frowned. "I don't know," she said. "I had really only just met all of them."

"Explain."

"I took a sail on a yacht, the *Mary Jane.*"

"Tell me all about it."

So once more Agatha told her story, but a bald account devoid of speculation.

He listened carefully. "What interests me, Mrs. Raisin, although you have not said anything about it, is how this friendship arose."

"They weren't friends," said Agatha impatiently. "Like I told you, they called me over to their table at The Grapevine, and then last night I had arranged to meet Mr. Lacey here for dinner at The Dome. Rose heard James asking for my table— he arrived first—and Rose claimed to be a friend of mine and urged him to join them."

Those hairy hands of his were removed from the table and clasped over his rotund stomach. Pamir was wearing a double-breasted suit, shirt, collar and tie. The heat did not seem to trouble him.

"Ah, yes, you and Mr. Lacey. You are staying here with him?"

"Yes."

"You are friends?"

"Yes, we are neighbours in the same village in the Cotswolds. That's an area in the Midlands—"

"I know," said Pamir.

"Your English is very good," said James.

"I was brought up in England and went to the London School of Economics. So, Mr. Lacey, you and Mrs. Raisin are neighbours. You arrived first. Mrs. Raisin joins you. Are you having, how shall I say, a liaison?"

"No," said James. "We're friends, that's all."

"So, Mr. Lacey, what has been happening to you since you first arrived on the island?"

So James told him of renting the villa from Mustafa.

"Mustafa has gone to the bad," said Pamir. His black eyes swivelled back to Agatha. "To return to your tourists. We have a lot of British residents here and I am well aware of the famous class differences. Mr. and Mrs. Debenham and their friend, Mr. Tembleton, are not of the class of Mrs. Wilcox and her husband. There is something in your story, Mrs. Raisin, which implies you were surprised by such a friendship."

"I was," said Agatha. "Olivia—that's Mrs. Debenham—is so snobby and she despised Rose. I've been wondering about that myself. Why on earth should such an unlikely lot get together, and why were George Debenham and Rose laughing together at Turtle Beach Cove?"

"You did not tell me about that."

Agatha told him, although she was aware of James glaring at her. "And Rose was actually intelligent," she said.

"Explain."

So Agatha expanded happily on how Rose would let slip about books she had read and then seem to remember her act. "If it was an act," she said finally.

There was another knock at the door. James went to answer it. He returned with a policeman who was carrying a sheaf of fax papers which he handed to Pamir.

Agatha sipped coffee with her eyes lowered, aware of James's angry eyes on her.

"Ah," said Pamir finally. "You lead an adventurous life, Mrs. Raisin. You and Mr. Lacey here were to be married, but the wedding was interrupted by the arrival of your husband, who was subsequently murdered. You planned to go to north Cyprus on your honeymoon, but while you were in hospital, Mrs. Raisin, recovering from an assault on you by the murderer, Mr. Lacey here left for Cyprus and then you followed him. If you will both forgive me saying so, in my experience people who lead violent and colourful lives are often violent themselves."

"Well, I'm not," said Agatha. "Why don't you go off and

grill that brothel-keeper, Mustafa, or does he bribe the police to stay away?"

"We'll deal with this murder first," said Pamir. "What we have here is two ill-assorted couples who mysteriously become friends very quickly. Now let us take the usual two motives—money and passion. Do you think George Debenham fell madly in love with Rose Wilcox?"

Agatha looked at James, who shrugged. She said, "No, there seemed to be no sign of that. Rose liked to flirt."

"But when Trevor saw Rose with George, he looked jealous?"

"Yes, he looked furious."

"Odd. Then they dine together, go to Famagusta together, and then dine together again. I must study the background on them all." He ruffled the sheaf of fax papers.

"James and I have had some experience of helping the police," said Agatha eagerly. "If I could just—" She reached out towards the fax papers. Pamir stuffed them in his breast pocket and got to his feet.

"I do not want this investigation hampered by amateurs," he said. "Try to enjoy your holiday and I shall see you both tomorrow."

James saw him out and then came back and leaned against the kitchen counter. "What a blabby little thing you are, *dear*. Why didn't you give him your knicker size when you were at it?"

Agatha cracked. She hurled her coffee-cup across the kitchen, where it smashed against the wall. "You cold, unfeeling bastard," she howled. She stumbled from the kitchen and ran up the stairs to her room and fell face-down on the bed.

The windows and shutters were open and a mild breeze blew in with a smell of pine, salt and vanilla. The Mediterranean was rough that day, and instead of falling on the beach in measured waves it roared steadily, as if there were a heli-

46

copter overhead. And so Agatha did not hear James come in.

He sat on the edge of the bed and lightly touched her hair.

"Come on, now, Agatha. This will not do. We'll go along to The Celebrity, where Trevor and Angus are staying, and see what we can find out." Agatha continued to sob. He went up the stairs and into the bathroom and soaked a towel with cold water. He came back and turned Agatha over and sponged her face.

"You'd better wear something cool." He searched through her clothes and picked out a loose flowered beach dress. He jerked her upright and started to unbutton her blouse. "Let's get this off for a start."

But Agatha was wearing a serviceable cotton brassiere and not one of the lacy French ones bought with seduction in mind, so she pushed him away, snarling, "Oh, leave me alone. I'll dress myself."

Soon they were driving off into the ferocious heat along to Lapta and so to the Celebrity Hotel. The hotel is rated four-star, but as Agatha walked into the reception and her jaundiced eye took in the amount of plush and gilt furniture, the chandeliers and the hot noisy carpets, she decided it was Middle Eastern four-star. No one at the reception desk had much English and so it took them some time to discover that Trevor and Angus had just checked out.

"Why can't they get someone who speaks bloody English?" raged Agatha. "They don't care about tourism in this country."

"Maybe that's why they don't rip them off, insult women and have the place full of lager louts," said James mildly. "Anyway, we ought to learn Turkish and stop whining about their lack of English."

"I wasn't whining. I was putting forward a reasonable criticism. For God's sake, why do you have to pick on me over every little damn thing?"

"This isn't getting us anywhere, and no, Agatha, you do not look beautiful when you're angry. I'll bet Trevor and Angus have gone to The Dome to join the Debenhams. We'll try there. We'll drop off at the villa first and pick up swim-suits and get a swim later."

But Agatha refused to speak to him. When they got back to their villa, the door was standing open.

"What the hell . . . ?" muttered James. He strode in. The noise of running water was coming from the kitchen.

They went into the kitchen. Jackie was scrubbing down the wall, which had been stained from the coffee-cup Agatha had thrown at it.

"I tried to phone you," said Jackie. "I hadn't left you enough clean towels and brought some round. What happened here?"

"The cup slipped out of my hand," said Agatha defensively.

Jackie's amused eyes looked at the wall and then back at Agatha. Then she took a dustpan and brush and cleared away the shards of broken china from the floor. "No one can talk of anything else but this murder," said Jackie. "You must have got an awful shock, Mrs. Raisin."

"Agatha."

"Agatha, then. Don't you think you should be having a quiet lie-down?"

"Perhaps you should," said James. "You're a bit over-wrought."

"I AM NOT OVERWROUGHT!" shouted Agatha.

Jackie wiped her hands on a towel, smiled at both of them and hurried off.

"You really must pull yourself together," said James severely. "Or I'll need to leave you behind."

But Agatha had no intention of being left behind. Whether she feared to be left out of the murder hunt or whether she feared that Olivia might charm James, she did not stop to think about. She went upstairs and washed her face but did not put on any make-up. There was no point. The heat and humidity would melt any make-up right off her face.

At the Dome Hotel, they learned that Trevor and Angus had checked in and were out at the pool. James bought a couple of tickets for the pool. "Did you bring any sun-block?" he asked Agatha. "You'll burn."

"I'll be all right."

"I'll buy you some across the road if you wait a moment."

"Don't fuss!" snapped Agatha.

They walked in silence through the lounges and out in the sunlight again towards the pool. Agatha changed in a cubicle. When she emerged, James was waiting for her, hard and lean and fit-looking in a pair of brief trunks. "They're over at the bar, all of them."

He pointed. At a table in full sunlight sat Trevor, Angus, Olivia, George and Harry.

They went over to join them.

"We're all a bit shell-shocked," said Olivia languidly. She was wearing a brief bikini. "Join me, James."

James sat down next to her. "How are you bearing up, Trevor?" he asked.

"I'll manage," said Trevor curtly. There were puffy bags under his eyes and he was burnt a dreadful shade of pink. There were already sun blisters on his shoulders but he seemed unaware of the heat.

"Poor, poor Rose," mourned Angus. "Who waud hae done such a thing to a bonnie lassie like that?"

"We phoned Trevor and Angus and told them to move here," said Olivia to James.

"Why?" asked Agatha, glaring, for Olivia had put a hand on James's thigh.

"Because people like us are brought up to help our fellow-man," said Olivia coldly. "Something that someone like you might not be aware of, Agatha."

Agatha felt that Olivia had pierced through the layers of Mayfair built up through the years to the Birmingham slum where Agatha had been brought up.

"Oh, piss off," said Agatha. "I'm going for a swim."

She was very conscious of her rear as she walked off. She hoped her bottom wasn't sagging. She really must pull herself together. She took a deep breath and jumped into the pool, expecting the shock of cold water, but the sea-water in the pool was warm. She swam energetically up and down until she felt calmer. She turned on her back to perform the backstroke and hit someone on the face. She rolled back over and found herself looking into a rather battered, but handsome middle-aged face.

"Sorry," said Agatha.

"It's all right," he said with a grin that revealed white teeth. "Couldn't have been hit by a more attractive lady."

"You're American?"

"No, Israeli. Here on holiday. You?"

"British. And on holiday as well."

"We can't talk very well paddling round each other like this," he said. "Let's sit at the edge of the pool for a bit."

"I'm Bert Mort," he said, extending a wet hand when they sat together at the edge, their feet in the water.

"Agatha Raisin," said Agatha, shaking his hand.

"I was brought up in Brooklyn," said Bert. "But I moved to Israel ten years ago and I've got a clothing business outside Tel Aviv."

"High-fashion?"

"No, T-shirts, holiday wear, things like that. Did you hear about the murder?"

"I was there."

"Jeez, that must have been awful. Tell me about it."

50

So Agatha did, hoping James was noticing her in the company of this good-looking man. She glanced across at James but his back was to her and he was talking to Olivia.

At last Bert said, "Why not join me for dinner tonight? Or is there a Mr. Raisin with you?"

"No, and I would like dinner. Where?"

"I'll meet you in the hotel dining-room at eight."

Agatha got up and said goodbye to her new friend and strolled back to the table. She felt all her old confidence restored.

"Olivia's given me some sun-block," said James. "Sit down, Agatha, and I'll put some on your shoulders. They're turning bright red."

As he stroked on the cream with an impersonal hand, Agatha said to Olivia, "I'm sorry I flared up like that. But I'm still tired. We had a grilling from the police this morning."

"Yes, so did we," said Olivia. "We're to go to Nicosia tomorrow for the official grilling."

"So are we," said Agatha. "But they must know none of us can have had anything to do with it."

"It's those damned foreigners and their knives," growled Harry Templeton.

"They don't think it was a knife," said Trevor. "They say it was something much thinner, like a kebab skewer."

Agatha had a sudden memory of Rose salaciously eating kebab off a skewer at The Grapevine. She wondered if a skewer had gone missing from The Grapevine.

James said they should leave. By the time Agatha had put her beachdress on, she could feel her shoulders beginning to burn painfully. She told James about her idea of checking at The Grapevine to see if a skewer was missing.

"I don't think that's much use," said James. "They sell them all over town. And any restaurant here is bound to have bundles of them in the kitchen. But we could go there for dinner tonight if you like."

"I've got a date."

They had reached the car. James turned and looked down at her.

"A date? Who with?"

"Some fellow I met at the pool."

He got into the car and slammed the door shut. Agatha went round to the passenger side and got in. They drove back to the villa in silence.

Agatha went straight to her room when they arrived. She lay down on the bed, suddenly tired and, lulled by the roar of the Mediterranean, fell fast asleep.

When she awoke, it was dark. She screwed her head around and looked at the luminous dial of her travelling alarm clock. Seven-thirty! She would need to rush.

There was no water in the bathroom and she felt sticky and grubby. She found a box of something called Fastwipes in her luggage for cleaning off make-up and used the whole box to wipe herself down. Her shoulders burnt like fire, but her face was getting a nice tan.

She eased a short silk dress over her shoulders. Her legs were red, not brown, and almost as sore as her shoulders, but the thought of putting on tights made her shudder.

She finally went down, calling to James. There was no reply and when she went outside, his car was gone.

She drove along the now familiar road through Karaoğlanoğlu, noticing the police were out looking for anyone speeding. Two cars had been stopped. Agatha cruised past them virtuously at a low speed. Down past the army barracks, then the Jasmine Court Hotel and on into Kyrenia and round the new one-way system and down to The Dome. Following the example of the locals, she parked on the pavement in a side street and walked to the hotel.

James was there, sitting with what she thought of coldly as "the murder suspects." She nodded to them curtly and sailed past them to a table overlooking the sea, where Bert was rising to greet her.

"I think I'll sit here," said Agatha brightly. "I like to watch the sea." She turned her chair around so that her face was to the sea and her back was to James.

"Have you been a widow long?" asked Bert after he had ordered wine.

"Not very long," said Agatha.

"And do you miss him?"

"No, it was a strange business. I had left him years ago and I thought he would have died of drink, but he only died a few months ago." Agatha did not want to say her husband had been murdered in case this new beau thought she might be responsible for the murder of Rose.

"What about you?" she asked.

"My wife died two years ago. I've been pretty lonely since then." He laughed. "And frustrated. I'm not one for casual affairs."

"Nor me," said Agatha, eyeing him speculatively and wondering what life would be like in Israel.

"When I saw you in the pool, do you know, I had this funny feeling I had known you a long time," said Bert. "Have some more wine."

Behind Agatha, Olivia brayed with laughter and said, "Oh, James, you are wicked."

Agatha held out her glass and smiled into Bert's eyes. "This is a very romantic setting," she said.

"Isn't it?"

The sea was calmer that evening and heaved itself up against the rocks below the hotel with rhythmic little splashes. Agatha had a heady feeling of elation. She was embarking on a new chapter of her life. She could forget all about Carsely, about James, about murder. Nothing really mattered except this handsome man whose eyes were glowing at her across the table.

There was a sudden rustling in the restaurant, then a silence. Agatha turned round. A beautiful young woman had entered the restaurant. She looked like a foreign film star. She had long black, glossy hair, which she wore down on her tanned shoulders. She was wearing a short white lace dress. Her long, long tanned legs ended in high-heeled strapped sandals. Her large brown eyes were rimmed with thick black lashes. The silence ended and there was a murmur of appreciation.

Bert looked as if he had been shot through the heart. "She is very beautiful, isn't she," asked Agatha uneasily.

He made a funny croaking sound. The vision was approaching their table.

"Surprise!" she cried.

Bert rose to his feet. "Barbara!" he said. "You're the last person I expected to see."

"I thought I'd join you earlier than I'd planned." She looked down at Agatha inquiringly.

"Oh, this is a tourist who's staying at the hotel—Mrs. Raisin."

Agatha looked up at the beauty, bewildered. "Your daughter, Bert?"

"I'm his wife," she said with a laugh. "Aren't you pleased to see me, Bert?" She turned to Agatha. "He wasn't expecting me until next week, but I thought I would surprise him."

Agatha stood up. "Please have my chair," she said stiffly.

"But you haven't finished your meal, Mrs. Raisin!"

"I see my friends over there. I've got something I want to talk to them about."

Agatha walked over, pulled out a chair and sat down between James and Olivia. A waiter brought over her half-eaten plate of kebab and rice and placed it in front of her.

"Who is that glorious creature?" asked Olivia.

"She's his daughter," lied Agatha, aware of James's cynical eyes on his face.

"Then it's a very incestuous relationship," cackled Olivia. "She's just leaned across the table and kissed him on the mouth!"

"Yes, and now they're holding hands," said James.

"I don't really know him," mumbled Agatha. "Maybe I was mistaken . . . because of the age difference, you know." Desperate to turn the conversation away from Bert, and feeling old and plain and unwanted, Agatha asked, "Any more news about the murder?"

George shook his head. "They'll probably tell us something tomorrow."

Agatha looked curiously at Trevor. He was drinking steadily. Beside him, Angus was sunk in gloom. In fact, thought Agatha, Angus looked more like the bereaved husband than Trevor.

Olivia turned to Agatha. "You told us on that yacht trip that you had investigated murders, Agatha. Are you going to investigate this one?"

"I might see what I can find out."

"Oh, mind your own business," said Trevor suddenly and truculently.

"But, why?" asked Olivia. "Don't you want to know who killed poor Rose?"

"Of course I want to know and I'll kill the bastard the minute I find out who he is. But I don't want some woman poking her nose in because she thinks it's some sort of game."

"Steady on, old boy," said George, putting a hand on Trevor's arm. Trevor shook him off. He got to his feet. "I'm sick of the lot of you," he said. He marched out of the restaurant, colliding drunkenly with a table as he went.

"Och, now," said Angus placatingly. "You've not to be minding him, Agatha. We're all in a state of shock. I'd better go and see if he's all right."

Angus left as well.

There was an uneasy silence.

Olivia looked suddenly subdued. "I think I'll make an early night of it." She got to her feet and her husband and friend rose as well. "See you at the cop shop tomorrow," said Olivia.

That left James and Agatha alone.

"I wonder," said Agatha, "if I wrote to Bill Wong whether he could send me back some background on all of them."

"Your letter would arrive in Mircester in about five days' time," said James. "But his reply might never reach you, or if it did, it would take about four weeks. The post from abroad goes through Mersin in southern Turkey, and I just don't know why it should take so long to get here but it does."

"Fax. I could fax him."

"You could, I suppose. Do you really think one of them is the murderer?"

"Well, it's odd," said Agatha. "Olivia was so snobby on that yacht trip. She despised them. I can understand George making a play for Rose. She was a sexy thing. But Olivia! Did she give you a hint as to why they all got so pally?"

"Nothing more than the sort of one-must-do-one's-bit-for-one's-fellow-man type of thing."

"But they all got friendly before the murder!"

"Fax Bill Wong if you like. But I think some drunk did it. There's a lot of drugs here and pretty freely available. Could have been done by someone stoned out of his mind who doesn't even remember now he did it. Let's go, or" he added maliciously, "do you want another word with your boy-friend?"

Agatha's eyes filled with angry tears.

"Come now," he said lightly. "A lot of women would be flattered that a man with a wife as beautiful as that would make a play for them."

Agatha scrubbed at her eyes. "I knew he was married," she lied.

"If you say so," said James. "Come along."

The next day the humidity had lifted. Clear blue skies, the calmest of seas, and the lightest of breezes.

The mountains towered up to the sky on one side of the road and the blue-green sea stretched all the way to Turkey on the other side. Agatha suddenly wished she were simply on holiday instead of being back in the grip of the James obsession and on the way to police headquarters in Nicosia.

When they drew up outside the police headquarters, Agatha began to have a feeling that the whole business was unreal, that it had never happened, that Rose would stroll round a corner, diamond rings flashing and shout, "Owya, Agatha?"

Olivia, Trevor, Angus, George and Harry were already there. They were to be interviewed separately, and to Agatha's dismay, James suggested that they meet up at the Saray Hotel afterwards for lunch and compare notes.

Agatha had taken the precaution of bringing along a book to read. Trevor was the first to be called, then Olivia, and then Agatha heard her own name being shouted out.

Pamir was sitting behind a large desk. A large portrait of Atatürk in evening dress stared down from behind the desk.

A policeman drew out a chair for Agatha on the other side of the desk. She sat down, suddenly nervous.

Pamir folded those fat hairy hands of his on the desk in front of him. He was wearing a chocolate-brown double-breasted suit and a wide tie with orange-and-yellow stripes. A large yellow silk handkerchief flowered from his top pocket.

"Now, Mrs. Raisin," he said, "if I can just take you through the whole thing again. You arrived at the disco."

"James began to dance with Olivia," said Agatha, "and I danced with Angus, but he danced on my feet so I suggested we sit down."

"And Rose Wilcox?"

"She was dancing with George, Mr. Debenham."

"How were they dancing. Close?"

Agatha frowned in concentration. Her eyes had been mostly on James. "They weren't dancing close," she said. "Disco dancing. Rose was shaking it all about and George was doing that sort of high-stepping jerky dance that middle-aged gentlemen do when they think they're being swingers. The music was very loud and the floor was crowded."

"Was Mrs. Wilcox making a play for anyone in particular? You have told me about Mr. Debenham. What about Mr. Lacey?"

"What about Mr. Lacey?" demanded Agatha, her eyes narrowing.

"Did Mrs. Wilcox, Rose, seem attracted by Mr. Lacey?"

"Not that I noticed," said Agatha huffily.

"Now we go to last night. You had dinner at The Dome, but not with Mr. Lacey or any of the others but with a visiting Israeli businessman, a Mr. Mort."

"What's that got to do with the murder?"

"I must examine all the relationships and you have a very peculiar relationship with Mr. Lacey. You were engaged to be married, nearly got married, had not your husband appeared on the scene. You follow him here, you both share the same villa, and yet you accept an invitation to dinner from Mr. Mort."

"It was just a friendly chat," said Agatha hotly. "He was waiting for his wife."

"A wife you did not know existed until she arrived."

"That's not true! Have you been watching me?"

"Mrs. Raisin, one of my colleagues happened to be in that restaurant last night. I had a little man-of-the-world chat with Mr. Mort this morning. He found you attractive and asked you for dinner under the impression, to quote him, that he was 'on to a good thing'. So you agreed to join him for dinner, for a date, although you are with Mr. Lacey."

"Anything that was between me and Mr. Lacey is dead," said Agatha furiously. "We are friends and neighbours, that's all."

He bent his head and made some notes. Then he raised his eyes and looked at her thoughtfully. "As I said, I must examine all the tensions in your relationships, you and the rest. And here we have two threesomes, two devoted husbands and two devoted friends. Jealousy could have been a motive."

"You'll need to ask them."

"Oh, I shall. Now either someone had enough medical experience to know where to stick that thin blade which killed Mrs. Wilcox, or it was a lucky blow. Do you have any medical training, Mrs. Raisin?"

"None."

"And Mr. Lacey?"

"None either."

"It looks like a premeditated crime." He leaned forward. "Someone was prepared. Perhaps someone knew of the lighting in that disco—that at moments when the ball overhead swung round it was quite black. Had any of the others been there before?"

"I just don't know," said Agatha wearily. "I barely knew them. But perhaps I could be of help to you. I have helped the police before. The clue to the murder must lie in their backgrounds, that is, if one of them did it. If I could just study—"

"No," said Pamir firmly. "No amateurs. I suggest you manage to have something of a holiday and put this behind you."

"Meaning I am not a suspect?"

"Everyone who was in that disco on the night of the murder is a suspect. You may go, but do not leave Cyprus yet. Send Mr. Lacey in."

Agatha would have given anything to hear what went on between Pamir and James. Was he asking them about their relationship? And what would James say?

Then she decided gloomily that James would probably just say, again, they were only friends and that for some reason Agatha had followed him to Cyprus, and she would appear a pathetic middle-aged woman chasing lost love.

When James finally emerged, Agatha suggested that they should have lunch in Nicosia alone, but James said they should all have lunch together.

"Why?" demanded Agatha.

"Don't you want to find out who did this?"

"Ye-es," said Agatha reluctantly, not being able to say that she only wanted to be alone with him.

At last they had all been interviewed and silently they walked across to the Saray Hotel and took the lift up to the restaurant at the top. The call to prayer sounded out over the red roofs of Nicosia as they sat down at one of the tables next to the window.

"Damned caterwauling," said Olivia crossly.

"It's a Muslim country," said Angus. "Well, ma friends, do ye think that's it?"

"If you mean, will they question us again," said James, "then I think they are bound to. They are sure one of us did it."

He glanced at Trevor, but Trevor was staring stonily out of the window at the minarets of the mosque.

"I'm beginning to think it's up to me to find out who did it," said Agatha, and then immediately regretted her words, because she immediately knew she sounded like an insensitive brag.

"Oh, all your stories about solving murders," said Olivia with a brittle laugh. "Are you sure you weren't fantasizing, dear?"

"No, I was not!" said Agatha hotly. "I have helped the police in Mircester in several cases."

"If you say so," said Harry Templeton with a slight sneer.

"Tell them, James," urged Agatha.

"It is true that Agatha, by blundering around in murder investigations, managed to prompt the murderer to show his, or her, hand," said James flatly.

Agatha looked at him in amazement. "If you were a woman, James, you would be called a bitch."

There was an awkward silence and then Trevor found his voice. "I wish the lot of you would realize I have lost my wife," he said flatly. "I think it was some local crazed on drugs. All I want to do is get the hell out of this buggering island and never see it again."

The waiter came up and they ordered food. Agatha studied Angus. Trevor had shown all the signs of being a very jealous husband and yet he had allowed this doting friend to join them on holiday. Why? Did he think Angus too old and too pompous to be any competition at all? Or had Angus paid for it?

She suddenly thought that she really ought to fax Bill Wong at Mircester Police Headquarters and ask him for the background on all of them.

Olivia decided her social skills were needed to guide them all through this awkward lunch. She encouraged James to talk about his book, and Angus to talk about what he did in his retirement and Harry to talk about farming. Trevor kept to a morose silence and somehow Olivia kept steering the conversation so that Agatha was excluded.

When they finally left the restaurant and were grouped on the pavement outside the Saray Hotel, Agatha linked her arm in James's and said firmly, "Well, goodbye. I would like to take a look at the covered market again."

She led James off. When they were clear of the others, Agatha said, "That was a nasty crack of yours about the way I solved those murders."

"I thought you were being insensitive with Trevor sitting there. Besides, if we're going to investigate this and you think one of them is a murderer, it's a good idea not to advertise what you're doing."

"Oh, Mr. Know-All!" Agatha stopped short in front of a jeweller's window. "Those Rolex watches look remarkably cheap."

"Pirated," said James curtly. "Probably only run for about a week. Do you really want to see the covered market again?"

"Not really. I wanted to talk to you without the others listening. Somewhere in their backgrounds must be some sort of clue to Rose's death. What if we fax Bill Wong from the Onar Village Hotel on the way back and ask him to dig something up?"

"Let's leave it for another day," said James cautiously. "They may find out something here and then we do not need to bother Mircester police. In fact, why don't we do some sightseeing and pack up a picnic tomorrow and go and have a look at some of the sights. We'll start with Saint Hilarion."

Agatha was still staring into the jeweller's window as he talked. She suddenly pressed his arm warningly. For behind them, and in the window, she saw the reflections of Olivia and party.

How long had they been standing there?

They swung round. "We thought we'd take a look at the covered market as well," said Olivia.

"We've changed our minds," said Agatha before James could speak. The weather was still very warm and Olivia was wearing a brief sun-dress which showed her excellent breasts. I wish it would start to freeze, thought Agatha.

"What about dinner tonight?" asked Olivia.

"There's a very good restaurant at Zeytinlik, just outside Kyrenia," said James to Agatha's dismay. "The Ottoman House. Eight o'clock?"

"Great. We'll see you there."

"Aye, we've got to stick together," said Angus.

"Why on earth did you say that?" demanded Agatha angrily as they walked away. "Surely we've seen enough of them for one day."

"You want to investigate, don't you?" demanded James, steering her round a cartful of watermelons. "What do we really know about Harry and Angus, apart from the fact that Harry is a farmer and Angus a retired shopkeeper?"

"If we faxed Bill Wong, we'd find out all we have to know," said Agatha sulkily.

"Bill Wong may be too busy to bother about a murder case in Cyprus. It's only a dinner, Agatha, and we have the rest of the day to ourselves."

But when they got back to the villa, it was three-thirty in the afternoon and James said he was going to write.

Agatha retired to her room and began to search through her clothes for something to outshine Olivia. There was a phone extension in her room. On impulse she threw a pile of brightly coloured clothes on the bed and dialled the number of the vicar's wife, Mrs. Bloxby.

"Agatha," said Mrs. Bloxby. "How are you getting on? We read about the murder in the newspapers."

Agatha told her all about it, looking out of the window at the blue Mediterranean and thinking how very far away the village of Carsely seemed.

"And has this murder brought you and James closer together?" asked the vicar's wife when Agatha had finished.

"Not really," said Agatha on a sigh. "You know James."

"Oh, Agatha, I wish you could meet a really warm-hearted man!"

"James *is* a warm-hearted man. He just doesn't know how to show his feelings!"

"He may not have any to show."

"That's not true!" said Agatha furiously.

The vicar's wife was contrite. "I didn't really mean to say that, Agatha. I mean, I should not have said that. I don't know what came over me. We miss you here. Do you know when you are coming back?"

Agatha glared furiously through the open window at the sea and took a deep breath of sweet-scented air. She hated Carsely and never wanted to go back there again. Why couldn't everyone mind their own business? "I don't know," she snapped.

"If only I had kept my big mouth shut," said Mrs. Bloxby to her husband later. "Poor Agatha."

The vicar peered at his wife over the tops of his spectacles. "I would not feel sorry for Agatha Raisin. In my opinion she and James Lacey thoroughly deserve each other."

FOUR

†

THE evening was warm and sticky, and dark clouds ob-
scured the moon. Agatha had put on full make-up, but as
they arrived at the restaurant in Zeytinlik, she could feel foundation and mascara beginning to melt. She was wearing a
black evening dress with a short skirt and high collar. As she
turned her head in the car to speak to James, she felt her
damp cheek brushing against her collar and knew immediately it was probably smeared with Vichy Camel foundation
cream. She was wearing tights. Her legs had still not recovered from their burning by the pool and the humidity was
making the hairs on her legs sprout dreadfully. She passed
a tentative hand across her upper lip but she had waxed it
before leaving and it still felt smooth. Oh, all the things that
careless youth takes for granted, like a slim figure, smooth
skin and a hair-free face! In that moment, she desperately
wished to be back in her late thirties—that was not asking
too much—when one could indulge in, say, a large piece of
cheesecake without feeling two minutes after it had been con-

sumed that one's knicker elastic was cutting off one's circulation.

The proprietors, Emine and Altay, gave them a welcome and ushered them to a table next to a fountain in the centre of the garden restaurant, where Olivia and party were already seated. Between sunburn and booze, Trevor's face looked as if it had been boiled. The food as usual was delicious, but Trevor complained loudly and drunkenly that he was tired of "this foreign muck" and would give anything for a good steak and kidney pie.

"This place used to be called Templos," said Olivia loudly to break the awkward silence which followed Trevor's outburst. "The Knights Templars were stationed here and it was a sort of market garden for Saint Hilarion Castle. Some even say there is a tunnel here somewhere that leads right up to the castle."

"I think that's an engineering feat that would surely be beyond the Crusaders," said Agatha.

"They built the castle up on top of the mountain," said Olivia, "so a tunnel wouldn't have been beyond them."

Agatha decided to change the subject. She did not like being contradicted. "I cannot understand why north Cyprus is not a recognized country," she said.

"It's all quite simple," said James. "They let the world forget about the massacres they endured, about the women and children in one village buried alive with their hands tied behind their backs. The Greek Cypriots have a very powerful propaganda machine and this side has little or nothing. If I were an emerging country, I would not waste money on guns or bullets, but I would hire a Madison Avenue public-relations company. I've talked to some members of the government here. 'Why don't you keep reminding the world of what you have suffered?' I asked. They say they only counter-attack."

"They have the UN here," said Angus.

"And what *is* the UN?" demanded James. "I'll tell you what their function is. To cost various countries a great deal of money so that their soldiers can stand around surveying ethnic cleansing. And what the hell am I talking about ethnic cleansing for? Genocide is the word. Hasn't the suffering of the Jews taught this damn world anything? Look at Bosnia!"

"What delicious lamb on the bone," said Olivia brightly. "Do try some, Trevor. Just like Mother used to make."

"My mother only made with the can opener," said Trevor.

What an ill-assorted lot we are, thought Agatha. Even me and James. He talks with such passion about politics but I can't get him to say one word about us. Passion, thought Agatha. Was that what was behind this murder? But George Debenham, thin and sallow like his wife, seemed always cool and detached. Then there was friend Harry Templeton, whose expression was usually hidden behind a pair of thick spectacles, and yet, in his way, Harry was almost a reflection of Angus, both being old and sagging and with white thinning hair. Perhaps there was a breed of elderly men who attached themselves to married couples.

"Were you ever married, Harry?" asked Agatha.

He blinked at her through his glasses and said, "Yes, but she died twenty years ago."

"And you, Angus?"

"Never found anyone to suit me," said Angus sadly. His Scottish accent was only slight when he forgot to thicken it. "If I could have met someone like Rose, it might have been a different matter." Agatha glanced quickly at Trevor to see how he had taken this declaration, but Trevor appeared to be once more sunk in gloom.

"And what about you, Agatha?" asked Olivia. "Rose told us she remembered reading about you. Your husband was murdered just as you were about to marry James here. It's a wonder he's forgiven you."

"He hasn't and won't, ever," said Agatha, her eyes suddenly filling with tears. "Excuse me." She rose to her feet and went to the toilet and leaned against the wash-hand basin. What is up with me? she thought. Is this the menopause?

Should I go on hormone-replacement therapy? Or maybe I need a good psychiatrist to tell me that my infatuation for James is because I'm sick in the head.

She walked wearily out of the toilet and back towards the table in the garden. Then she stopped stock-still and gazed in amazement at the entrance to the restaurant.

A small man with fine hair and a thin, sensitive face was standing there, looking vaguely about him.

Agatha walked towards him. "Charles."

Sir Charles Fraith, Baronet, focused on her. "Funny thing," he said, "I was just thinking about you, Agatha. Folks at the hotel were talking about some Englishwoman being murdered and you crossed my mind."

Agatha had been part of a murder investigation when a rambler had been found dead on Sir Charles's land.

"Do you want to join us?" Agatha indicated her party, who were all staring at them.

"That's that chap Lacey," said Charles. "That's the one you nearly married. Odd bunch of people with him. No, I don't think I want to join them."

"What are you doing here, Charles?"

"Just a little holiday. You're here with Lacey? Honeymoon?"

"No, we're just friends."

"Oh, in that case, let's go somewhere for a drink."

"Don't you want to eat?"

"No, I was just cruising the highways and byways, looking for a cool place to have a drink."

"You'd best come over and say hullo," said Agatha, who was looking forward to introducing this baronet to Olivia.

"I don't think so, Agatha. You know what will happen. They'll all come with us. Let's just drift off."

Suddenly the thought of just walking away with Charles and going for a quiet drink somewhere seemed wonderful.

James had engaged Olivia in conversation, not wanting Agatha to know that they were all awaiting her return impatiently. He had not recognized Charles, who was slightly hidden by a palm; he only knew that Agatha was talking to some man. When he looked up again, Agatha and her companion had gone.

Ten minutes later Agatha and Charles were sitting at an outdoor café near the Dome Hotel.

Charles ordered brandy sours for both of them and leaned back in his chair and gazed vaguely out to sea.

"I heard you'd got married," said Agatha.

"Engaged. Didn't work. No chemistry. Sarah was very attached to her parents. Very worthy people, but her father was the sort of man who puts logs on *my* fire. Know what I mean?"

"Sort of," said Agatha, suddenly getting a picture of a solid middle-class family, foreign in their ways to the aristocratic Charles.

"They liked giving very long dinner parties with such boring people. I used to sit there thinking, when will this evening end? Bring on the cheese. Oh, please God, bring on the cheese."

"So you broke off the engagement? How's Gustav?" Gustav had been Charles's manservant.

"Left me because of the engagement. Terrible snob, Gustav."

"Where is he now?"

"Maître d' in some classy hotel in Geneva."

"Did you replace him?"

"No. Can't have servants these days. Anachronism. Get women in from the village to clean, hire a catering company if we've a lot of people at the weekend. So what about this murder?"

Agatha told him all about it, feeling as she did so that every time she talked about it the whole thing became more unreal.

His pale eyes swivelled from the sea to her face. "So what about it? Are you hot on the trail?"

"I'm not," said Agatha gloomily. "In fact, I should be back there with James trying to find out more about them all. I thought of faxing Bill Wong, you know, my friend at Mircester police, asking him for some background, but James said to wait."

"I'll ask The Dome to send a fax if you like."

Damn James, thought Agatha. Why shouldn't she act on her own initiative?

"I haven't got a typewriter here, or computer," said Agatha.

"Write it by hand. I mean, it's not the Epistle to the Romans, is it? Just a few lines."

"I'll do it!" said Agatha.

"Good girl," said Charles, appearing to lose interest.

"So how are things back home?" asked Agatha, wondering now what James was making of her disappearance, and feeling uncomfortably that she had behaved badly.

"Oh, same as ever. That's a very pretty girl over there."

Agatha had the ordinary feminine irritation of being asked to admire some woman by a male companion. And she had walked off and left the field to Olivia. But as she was eager for Charles to arrange that fax to Bill Wong, she did not want to hurry him over his drink.

At last he signalled to the waitress and paid the bill.

The manager was still on duty and agreed to send a fax. Agatha wrote out her request on a piece of paper, asking for any reply to be sent to her at The Dome to await collection.

"I will put the charge on your bill," said the manager to Charles.

"It's not my fax," said Charles. "Mrs. Raisin will pay."

"Where are you staying, Mrs. Raisin?" asked the manager. "My accountant will send the bill to you."

Agatha wrote down her address.

"Well, I'm off to bed," said Charles, stifling a yawn.

"Aren't you going to run me home?" asked Agatha. "I went to the restaurant in James's car."

"Too tired. I'll get you a cab."

Charles ordered a cab for her at reception and nodded to her and walked off.

The receptionist said, "It is a very busy night. Your cab will be about ten minutes."

"I'll wait in the bar," said Agatha.

She walked through to the bar and stopped short on the threshold. Charles, with another brandy sour in his hand, was talking to a group of Turkish women. Agatha felt rejected all round—by James, by Charles.

She returned to the reception desk and waited until her cab arrived. But when she got back to the villa, it was to find the place in darkness, and James had the keys. She told the cab driver to take her to the Ottoman House Restaurant, only to find that they had all left half an hour before. Thinking she might have missed James on the road, she went back to the villa to find it still in darkness. Wearily she told the driver to take her back to The Dome.

James was not there and the others were not in their rooms. Where had they gone?

She sat down on a chair in the reception area and stared bleakly around.

"Still here?" asked Charles, walking up to her.

"Still here," echoed Agatha dismally. "James is still out somewhere and he has the keys."

"It's late. I'm off to bed." Charles hesitated. "Got two beds. You can have the other one if you like."

"I wouldn't mind that," said Agatha gratefully. "I'm tired of running around."

"Come along, then," he said, heading for the lift. "Just don't use my toothbrush."

Once in his room, he threw her a pair of pyjamas. "You can wear those and use the bathroom first."

Agatha washed and changed into the pyjamas. "You're in the bed by the window," said Charles when she emerged. "I hope you don't snore."

I don't think so," said Agatha. Tears started to her eyes. "Well, if I do, no one's ever told me."

"Have a good cry," he said. "Nothing like a bloody good cry. Then we'll have a drink and you'll sleep like a log."

He went into the bathroom. Agatha stared bleakly ahead. All in that moment, she longed to be back home in her cottage in Carsely with English rain drumming down on the thatch, secure with her cats sleeping at the end of the bed. What on earth was she doing sharing a foreign hotel room with this odd baronet?

He emerged from the bathroom finally, wearing a pair of paisley-patterned pyjamas. He flung open the windows and shutters. "There's at table out on the balcony, Aggie. Come and take a pew."

Agatha sat out on the balcony. The air was warm and sweet and the sound of the sea soothing.

"I can't mix brandy sours," he said, returning with a bottle and two glasses. "But at least I've got the brandy. It's local stuff but not bad."

They drank silently and then he said, "What was all that about?"

"What about?"

"You were nearly in tears, Aggie."

"It's Agatha."

"I like Aggie. I shall call you Aggie, and since you are in my room and drinking my brandy, I can call you what I like."

Slightly tipsy now, Agatha began to talk. She told him all about James, about her relationship with James, about her obsession with James.

"I had a crush on a girl like that when I was seventeen," he said when she had finished. "That's what it's like, Aggie. A teen-age crush."

"I didn't expect you to understand," said Agatha sadly.

"Have you ever considered," he said, tilting his brandy glass in the moonlight and watching the liquid, "that there is something up with the man to keep you hanging around like this?"

"I behaved badly. He won't forgive me."

"Then he should stop jerking your chain. All he had to do was tell you that you should not have followed him out here, that it is all over, and get lost, Aggie."

She bent her head. "I think he still loves me."

"Dream on. And talking of dreams, let's go to bed."

Agatha sighed, drained her glass and followed him into the bedroom. Somehow, even in his pyjamas, Charles looked as neat and impersonal as if he were wearing a business suit.

She got into bed. What a mess! Her head swam from all she had drunk.

"Move over," she heard Charles say.

"What?"

"Move over." He edged into the bed next to her and took her in his arms.

"What are you doing?" demanded Agatha.

"What do you think?"

He bent his head and kissed her slowly. Oh, well, just one kiss, thought Agatha drunkenly. It was all very soothing and sensuous and not quite real. He had forgotten to put on the air-conditioning and the windows were still open. He kissed her for quite a long time before he took her pyjamas off and Agatha's last sane thought was, oh, what the hell.

She awoke at five in the morning with the telephone ringing shrilly. Charles answered it. She heard him say, "Yes, James, she's here. She had nowhere to go, so I let her use the spare bed."

"He's coming up," said Charles after he had replaced the receiver. He got out of bed and rapidly put on the pyjamas he had discarded.

Agatha ran for the bathroom, where she had left her clothes. She turned on the shower and washed herself hurriedly, dried, and then put on her clothes. Outside she could hear the sound of voices. She looked anxiously at her face in the mirror, but it showed no signs of love-making.

She went out into the hotel room. "So there you are," said James cheerfully. "What a scare you gave us! Police all over the place looking for you."

"Where were you?" asked Agatha, avoiding looking at Charles. "I went to the villa, to the restaurant, but there was no sign of anyone."

"We all went on to a bar. Thanks for looking after her, Charles. I gather that must have been you at the restaurant. Why didn't you say hullo?"

"My pleasure," said Charles smoothly, ignoring the last question. "Now, if you both don't mind, I'll get some more sleep. I'm quite exhausted. Must be the sea air."

James led the way. Agatha turned in the doorway and looked back at Charles, but his neat features were closed and impersonal.

Men, thought Agatha Raisin. I'll never understand them.

Rose Macaulay described Saint Hilarion as "a picture book castle for elf kings" and it is supposed to have inspired the animators of *Snow White*. Sited on its craggy eyrie, 2,400 feet above the plain, Saint Hilarion is best known as the honeymoon castle of Richard the Lionheart. Saint Hilarion consists of three distinct sections on different levels. The highest part of the castle, reached by very steep worn steps, is the Tower of Prince John. Signs on the road up to the castle proclaim in multiple languages that photography is forbidden, but no one seems to pay any attention to that, in the same way as the locals pay no attention to either speed limits or parking restrictions.

Agatha climbed out of the car in the car-park the following afternoon and looked all around. Far below her on one side stretched the blue Mediterranean; on her other side, the ruins of the castle reared up against cloudless skies. There was a smell of pine, and cicadas chattered with their sewing-machine busyness.

James had let her sleep late and had been unusually quiet on the journey up the long winding road to the castle. Agatha felt guilty about having slept with Charles. What had come over her? And what had come over him? Charles had not shown any sign earlier in the evening of having been attracted to her in any way. He probably regarded her as a convenient lay. Agatha blushed.

"Your face is all red," said James. "Is it the heat?"

"Yes, yes," said Agatha fretfully. "The sun is very strong up here."

They walked together out of the car-park, past a small café and up steep steps towards the first part of the castle. Agatha felt bone-weary. She stumbled slightly. James caught her arm with unexpected roughness and said sharply, "I didn't know you and Charles were such buddies."

"We're not," said Agatha, jerking her arm away. "I only saw as much of him during that case as you did."

"That's what I thought. So why did you just walk off with him last night?"

"He took a look at the company and didn't like what he saw, so he asked me for a drink," said Agatha defensively. "What's up with that?"

"There's nothing up with that. Why did you just walk off with him? Oh, I know, my snobby little friend. He's a baronet."

"It wasn't that," raged Agatha. "I just wanted to get away from the lot of you!"

"Leaving me to find out what I could. One minor aristo crosses your path, Agatha, and you're off and running."

"That's not true. I sent a fax off to Bill Wong."

"What?"

"I sent a fax to Bill from The Dome. Charles saw the manager for me and he—"

"And you didn't think to tell me?"

"How could I? You weren't there."

"And didn't you think to get a taxi? There was no need surely to climb into a comparative stranger's bed."

"I climbed into the spare bed. I had already been out to the villa twice. You weren't there. Was I supposed to cruise back and forwards all night, waiting for you to get home? Isn't there a spare set of keys?"

He fished in his pocket and handed her a ring of keys. "Jackie called with these this morning. That's the front door, that the back, that's the door off the upper terrace. Okay?"

"Thank you," said Agatha stiffly. "Are we going to stand here all day in this heat or are we going to get on and see this lump of rubble?"

They walked grimly on and upwards.

At last Agatha cried, "I've got to sit down for a moment."

She sank down onto a wall in the shade. James sat down beside her and stared at the ground at his feet. The atmosphere became heavy with unspoken accusation. Agatha pulled her guidebook out of her handbag and began to read aloud:

"This upper ward is reached up a steep path (stout shoes recommended), leading westward along the face of the crag and past an enormous open reservoir, which must have held enough water to last the inhabitants for many months. Veer right at the top to enter the upper enceinte through a Frankish arch. To the north of the entrance are more kitchens, and at the far (west) end of the upper plateau, a long narrow building which formed the Queen's apartments; on the upper floor is the elegant 'Queen's window,' retaining some of the original tracery and benches."

"Did you sleep with him?" James's voice cut across this travelogue.

"Don't be silly, James," said Agatha. "Let's go."

"Go yourself," he said moodily.

She got to her feet and began to climb upwards, her thoughts in a turmoil. James was behaving like a jealous man, but why? It was not as if he had any interest left in her, or if he had, he was putting on a very good act not to show it. Oh, why had she let Charles make love to her? Hot tears started to Agatha's eyes. She was beginning to feel thoroughly ashamed of herself.

At this higher level, there were no tourists other than herself. She could hear them arriving below in the car-park, but for the moment it seemed as if she had this section all to herself.

She walked to one of the windows and looked out. From her eyrie, the land dropped precipitously, tumbling down in a series of crags, broken rock, pine trees and scrub. The air was sweet and fresh. She felt a great peace descend on her. Just for this moment she could forget about murder and James and Charles and all the other messy complications of her muddled life.

She put her handbag on the ground at her feet and stood with both hands leaning on the warm stone at either side of the window, wondering if Queen Berengaria had stood just here and looked at this view, if she had loved Richard of England as she, stocky middle-aged Agatha, loved her James.

And then, without turning round, she became aware of anger filling the room and knew someone had entered and that someone was probably James. She stiffened her back and braced her hands on either side of the window, awaiting more questions about Charles.

That action was to save her life.

She received a vicious shove in the back which nearly sent her flying through the window and down to her death on the rocks below. She screamed out desperately, "Help! Murder! Help!" and her voice rang out over Saint Hilarion and sent birds flying from the trees on the hillside.

James heard that scream and came hurtling up the steps

and into the room where Agatha was slowly turning around, her face white.

"You," said Agatha. "Was it you?"

"What happened? Why did you scream?"

Other tourists came running and crowded into the room as well. "Someone pushed me in the back," said Agatha, beginning to shake. "Someone tried to push me to my death."

The room was filling up with soldiers, taxi drivers and more tourists.

And then a policeman pushed to the front of the crowd, followed by a tour guide. Agatha repeated again what had happened to her and the guide translated.

"You are to go with this policeman to the café in the carpark," said the guide, "and wait."

James helped Agatha out and down the steps. The crowd followed, chattering in a mixture of languages.

James ordered a brandy for Agatha. "Tell me again what happened," he asked gently.

Agatha took a sip of brandy. "I was standing there, looking out of that window. If I hadn't had my arms braced against the sides, that push in the back would have sent me to my death. I thought it was you, James."

"Why me?"

"I thought you were still angry with me. I sensed the anger in the room behind me. I thought it was you. That's why I didn't turn round." She looked at him, her eyes suddenly dilating. "What about Olivia and the rest? Are they here?"

"I haven't seen any of them. But they wouldn't dare—"

"They were right behind us at that jeweller's in Nicosia when we were discussing going to Saint Hilarion, when we were talking about faxing Mircester for details on their backgrounds."

"I didn't see any of them, and if it were one of them, they would surely have had to pass me on the road up."

"Why is it always me?" moaned Agatha. "Why doesn't someone have a go at you?"

"Because I don't interfere so noisily."

The wail of sirens sounded louder from the road below as more police headed their way.

And then Pamir arrived, nattily dressed as usual, and not appearing to feel the heat.

Wearily Agatha went through her story again.

But when he took her back over the events of the day before, carefully noting that Agatha thought she had been overheard when she said they were going to Saint Hilarion but making no mention of faxing Mircester, he began to ask about last evening. They had had dinner together at the Ottoman House, Did anything happen there?"

"You'll need to ask James," said Agatha. "I left."

"Ah, yes." He consulted some notes. "The police were informed that you had not returned home and then you were found at The Dome in the bedroom of Sir Charles Fraith."

"Sir Charles is an old friend," said Agatha. "It was a surprise to see him again. He suggested we go for a drink and we did. When I left him and returned to the villa again, James was not there. I went back to the restaurant but everyone had gone. Then I went to The Dome and they weren't there either. Charles said he had a spare bed in his room and I was very tired and so I accepted his offer."

Pamir's fathomless eyes switched to James. "Were you jealous?"

"Of what?" demanded James.

"Of Mrs. Raisin here. Of her behavior. First she has dinner with a business man and now she shares the bedroom of an Englishman who is not you."

"I have no reason to be jealous," said James. "I am used to Agatha's erratic behaviour."

"Why did you leave your friends without saying where you were going?" asked Pamir, consulting his notes again.

"Because Sir Charles did not want to meet them and may I remind you, they are not friends of mine. We have only been brought together because of this murder."

"But Mr. Lacey appears to like them."

"Until this murder is solved," said James, "I am a suspect. I thought if I spent some time with them, I could find out more about them."

"Ah, the amateur English detective. Like Mrs. Raisin here. But Mrs. Raisin was more curious about Sir Charles."

"Stop making me sound like the Whore of Babylon," shouted Agatha, her face red. "Charles is an old friend. I was startled to see him. I do not like the Debenhams, if you want the truth, and seized on the opportunity to escape. I know what you are going to ask and no, I did not tell James where I was going. He is not my husband!"

"But very nearly was," murmured Pamir. "Right, let's go through it all again from when you left police headquarters."

Agatha looked appealingly at James. Surely she had gone through enough. She had nearly been killed and yet he sat there with an impassive face, letting this policeman grill her.

So both told their stories again. James said that after Agatha had left and they had finished their meal, they had gone on to a bar for drinks. They had not talked about the murder out of respect for Trevor's grief.

At last they were free to go. Agatha stood up shakily. James put a hand under her arm and guided her to the car.

"We still have the picnic," he said. "Do you want to go back to the villa and rest?"

Agatha said, "Forget about the picnic, James. All I want to do is sleep."

But when they turned into the narrow road leading to their villa, James slammed on the brakes and reversed back out into the main road and sped off. "Press," he said bitterly. "The British press have arrived and I don't feel like coping with them."

"Me neither," said Agatha. "Find a nice cool picnic spot and maybe I'll get a sleep in the open."

James looked in the driving mirror. "They're pursuing us."

"What can we do?"

"Lose them."

He swung off the road and accelerated up towards the mountains, round a bend and shot off into a field behind a stand of trees and cut the engine. Out on the road, they heard the press cars roar past. James reversed and went back down to the coast road, through Kyrenia and then down onto another coast road.

"Not much of a beach," he said, stopping at last. "But at least there's no one around."

He spread out the picnic on a flat rock beside the water: bread, black olives, cheese, cold chicken and a bottle of wine.

Agatha thought she would not be able to eat, but after the first bite of chicken decided she was very hungry.

She lay back after she had eaten and closed her eyes. "I didn't sleep with Charles," she said. "Honestly." Agatha thought privately that what she had done with Charles could hardly be described as sleeping.

"I know," said James quietly.

Well, I probably won't see Charles again, thought Agatha, and then fell asleep.

James watched her for a moment and then went to the car and got a straw hat which he placed gently over her sleeping face.

When they returned to the villa, the press had gone. "There's a news in English about now," said James. "Let's see if there's anything about the murder."

The local TV station was usually long on words spoken in badly accented English by some pretty newscaster and short on pictures. But to Agatha's amazement they had pictures this time—of a press conference at The Dome. Lined up behind a table were Olivia, George, Harry, Angus and Trevor.

Trevor, unlike his usual taciturn self, gave an emotional and heart-broken plea to the people of north Cyprus to help the police discover who had murdered his precious wife, Rose. He then relapsed into noisy sobs.

Olivia then took over, Olivia in a simple black gown and pearls and with her face as cunningly made up into a mask of grief as that of Princess Di's during her famous *Panorama* interview. With the sharp eyes of pure jealousy, Agatha took in the pale make-up, the carefully arranged wispy hair-style and the shadows painted under the eyes.

With a break in her voice, lowered a register, Olivia said she had only known Rose a short time but they had become firm friends. "She was so full of life," said Olivia, "and to see such a life snuffed out is a tragedy."

Angus then put in his bit in an accent so broadly Scottish it was almost unintelligible. He said Rose was a "puir wee broken burdie."

"Pass the sick-bag," snarled Agatha.

"Shh!" admonished James, turning up the volume. George spoke next, in a gruff, embarrassed voice about how they all missed Rose. Only Harry Templeton remained silent.

"And now the weather," said the newscaster.

"I wonder when that conference was," said James. "I mean, if they were all at a press conference they could hardly be up at Saint Hilarion trying to push you out of a window. Let's go and find out."

"They might have told us what they were up to," complained Agatha.

"They could hardly do that as we haven't seen them. Let's go."

When they arrived in The Dome, the manager approached them and said, "I have a fax for you, Mrs. Raisin.

"Now we'll find out all about them," said Agatha excitedly.

But the fax from Bill Wong said only, "Call me at my home number."

"Rats," said Agatha.

"I see his point," said James. "Forget about here for the

moment. We'd best get back and phone." He turned to the manager. "When was that press conference here—about the murder?"

"At four-thirty this afternoon." That let no one out. The attack at Saint Hilarion had been at one o'clock.

"Can't we phone from here?" Agatha asked James.

"Yes, but too expensive."

Back they went to the villa. "It's early over there," said James as he picked up the phone. "There's two hours' difference. What's the number?"

Agatha fished a small leather-bound book out of her handbag and then took the phone from James. "He's *my* friend," she said. "I'll phone."

Mrs. Wong answered. "My Bill's just dropped in is having a cup of tea. You'll need to call back."

"I'm phoning from Cyprus," howled Agatha.

Fortunately the receiver at the other end was taken from Mrs. Wong and Bill's voice came on the line. "You can't keep away from murder, can you?" he said cheerfully.

"Oh, Bill," said Agatha thankfully, "did you get anything on any of them?"

"I shouldn't be doing this," he said, "and don't you ever let anyone know where you got your information from. Here goes."

James paced up and down impatiently as Agatha listened and took notes. Then Agatha finally said, "Well, thanks a lot. That's given me something to think about. No, I won't get into trouble. Yes, I found James. He's here. What? No, no, no."

James wondered what that no, no, no had been in answer to.

Agatha finally rang off and turned and looked triumphantly at James. She began to tell him what she had learned. Trevor's plumbing business was on the skids and the receivers were shortly to be called in. Angus was a very rich retired man who had owned a chain of shops in Glasgow. George Debenham was also in financial trouble, having gambled unwisely on the stock exchange. Friend Harry was a comfortably-off farmer, no debts there. Rose Wilcox was extremely rich in her own right, the result of three previous marriages, the last of which had left her a very wealthy widow before she married Trevor.

"So does Trevor inherit now she's dead?" asked Agatha, her eyes gleaming. "And why wouldn't she bail his business out if she was that wealthy?"

"The simplest way will be to ask Trevor, but I'd like to get him away from the others. Let's leave it until tomorrow, Agatha. We'll go in early in the morning and suggest he might like to take a drive with us. Leave it until tomorrow."

But Agatha fretted. "Bill might know," she said, "and have forgotten to tell me."

But when she phoned Bill's number again, Mrs. Wong told her acidly that her son had gone over to see his new girlfriend—"such a nice *young* lady."

So that was that. James said he was tired and hungry and he would cook them both something to eat.

Agatha sat staring into space. This was not how she would have imagined it to be. Her dreams had turned upside-down. No lingering romantic kisses beside the Mediterranean—except from Charles. Every time she thought of that episode with Charles, she felt hot and uncomfortable. How could she have let one man make love to her when she was in love with another? Because, said a nagging voice in her head, maybe you've never really been in love with James but with an imaginary James. The imaginary, or dream, James was always doing and saying the right things while the real James was as cold and distant as ever. Agatha gave a broken little sigh. Her obsession with James seemed to be waning as each day passed.

Over dinner James suddenly said, "I would like to get even with Mustafa for cheating me. I'll bet he's dealing in drugs. You don't have all those villains around just because you're running a brothel."

"Could be dangerous," said Agatha.

"So's poking about in a murder investigation, but it hasn't stopped you yet."

"Oh, well, I'll help you."

"Not this one," said James firmly. " 'I'll deal with Mustafa myself."

FIVE

†

WHEN Agatha went downstairs in the morning, she found a note on the kitchen table from James. It said briefly, "Gone off on some private business. Be back around lunchtime."

Agatha cursed and crushed the note into a little ball and shied it into the rubbish bin. They were no longer a team, she thought bitterly. She made herself a cup of coffee and sat down at the kitchen table and gloomily revised in her mind all James's coldnesses, all his snubs, and all his lack of affection, until she was perfectly sure she had no feelings left for him at all.

Then she decided to go into Kyrenia and do some investigating for herself. The day was a washed-out milky grey, with wreaths of mist hiding the tops of the mountains. It was very warm and humid.

She parked in a side street and walked down to the Dome Hotel. English tourists with high fluting voices came and went outside the hotel. North Cyprus seemed to be living up to its reputation of being the last genteel watering-hole along the Mediterranean.

Neither Olivia nor the rest were in their rooms. She went to the dining-room. A few people were having a late breakfast but they were not among them. But over at the window sat Charles, holding a coffee-cup between his slim fingers and gazing dreamily out to sea.

Agatha hesitated and then, with a little shrug, she walked towards his table. He looked up.

"Morning, Aggie," he said. "Where's your guard-dog?"

"If you mean James, he's gone off somewhere on his own. Have you see the Debenhams or the bereaved husband?"

"You've missed them. They had breakfast. Then they said something about going to Bellapais."

"What's that?"

"It's a place immortalized by Lawrence Durrell in his book *Bitter Lemons*. There's a Gothic abbey there. I'll drive you there. Got nothing else to do. In fact, I'm getting a bit bored. Thought of going home."

Agatha sat down opposite him. "Why did you sleep with me?"

"How old-fashioned you sound. You mean, why did I have sex with you? Put it down to brandy and moonlight on the Med."

Agatha looked at him curiously. "And the memory doesn't embarrass you?"

He looked at her in surprise. "Not a bit of it, Aggie. I enjoyed myself immensely. Want coffee or want to go?"

"May as well go," said Agatha somewhat sulkily. She felt a gentleman would have professed to have had some sort of affection for her.

Once in his rented car, Agatha fished out her guidebook and looked up Bellapais. "What does it say?" asked Charles.

"The Abbaye de la Paix was founded circa 1200 by Aimery de Lusignan for the Augustine monks forced to leave their Church of the Holy Sepulchre in Jerusalem by the Sara-

86

cens. The abbey was sometimes called the White Abbey from the colour of their habits. King Hugues (1267 to 1284) was a major benefactor of the abbey, which grew in size and importance to the extent that the Archbishop of Nicosia had trouble asserting his authority over it, until the Genoese invasion of 1372. In that year its treasures were looted, and the abbey never regained its previous glory. Under the Venetians the abbey declined further, in both prosperity and morality. By the sixteenth century it is recorded that many of the monks had wives, in some cases more than one . . ."

"Enough," said Charles. "I'll find out the rest when I get there."

"Did you hear what happened to me at Saint Hilarion?" asked Agatha.

"I heard someone tried to push you out of a window. Probably an enraged tourist, Aggie. Were you reading out of your guidebook at the time?"

"No," said Agatha crossly. "I was in deadly peril."

"This is becoming a tourist trap," said Charles, as they entered the village of Bellapais. "Look at all those holiday villas. Where's the abbey? I think I've missed a turn somewhere."

Agatha consulted her book again. "It says here the ruins are reached by a turning to the right, signposted for Dogankoy and Beylerbeyi off the main coastal road in the eastern outskirts of Girne. Girne is the Turkish name for Kyrenia."

"I know, dear heart. Lecture me no further. I will find it."

Soon they were parked at the abbey in the shadow of a tourist bus.

They walked through the south-west entrance under an arched and fortified gateway.

"I forgot to look for their car," said Agatha.

"Whose?"

"The Debenhams, friends and Trevor. That's why I'm here."

"Well, I want to see the cloisters," said Charles, striding

ahead, a very English figure in blazer and white slacks, white panama hat, white shirt and striped cravat.

Agatha followed slowly, not wanting to run after him like a pet dog.

Fragments of delicate arches surrounded the cloisters, warm and humming with insects in the heat. The mist had lifted and a golden sunlight flooded everything. Agatha, wondering idly where Charles had got to, was looking up at the carved bosses and corbels of the vaulting which featured human and animal heads, rosettes and the Lusignan coat of arms when a harsh voice behind her said, "So it's you, snooping around as usual."

Agatha gasped and swung round. Trevor stood there, his hands clenched into fists, his unhealthily pink face full of menace.

"Look," he said, thrusting his head forwards, "it's my wife that's dead, gottit? And I don't want no amateur busybody like you poking her nose in and getting under the feet of the police."

Agatha took a step backwards. "See here, Trevor," she said in the gentle tone of one who hopes to turn away wrath, "you are grieving and upset. But you must see that every bit helps. I have had some experience—"

Trevor took her by the shoulders and shook her. "Bug out," he shouted, "or it'll be the worse for you!"

"Leave her alone!"

Charles's calm voice came from behind them.

Trevor released Agatha and turned and stumbled away.

"You all right?" asked Charles.

"A bit shaken," said Agatha. "I thought he was going to punch me. He threatened me."

"Did he now? Why?"

"He said if I didn't stop investigating it would be the worse for me."

"Was he drunk?"

"I don't know," said Agatha wretchedly. "I wish James were here."

"Well, he isn't. Where is he?"

"He's angry with his old fixer, Mustafa. Mustafa cheated him over the rental of a house. He's a brothel-keeper but James thinks he might be running drugs."

"I say, this isn't England. The silly man doesn't want to get into that or he'll end up floating in Kyrenia Harbour."

"Oh, James can take care of himself. It looks as if it might have been Trevor who murdered Rose. For her money, you know."

"No, I don't know. Tell me."

Agatha hesitated. Such background information as she had should only be discussed with James. James would be furious if she disclosed all their secrets to Charles. But she was shaken and Trevor had frightened her and James wasn't there, only Charles, cool and inquisitive. So she told him all about Trevor's financial difficulties, and how she wondered why Rose, who was rich, had not bailed his firm out of its difficulties.

"I think we should find Trevor and the others and ask him in front of them why he threatened you," said Charles. "We'll keep his financial difficulties in reserve. If he knows you've contacted the police about him, he'll go ape."

They wandered through the rest of the abbey, refectory, undercroft, chapter house and dormitories among throngs of tourists—British, German and Israeli. But of Trevor there was no sign.

"If he's with the rest, they might have gone to some bar in the village," suggested Charles. "We'll look there."

They drove back to the village of Bellapais, parking in a car-park next to the Tree of Idleness Restaurant and then wandering through the narrow streets until Agatha saw two rented cars with the Atlantic sticker on the rear window outside a café. She peered through the glass. "They're all there.

Maybe I should get back and find James before I say anything."

"He's not your husband, father or keeper," said Charles, giving her a gentle shove in the back. "In you go."

Trevor, pink and sullen, was drinking beer. Olivia and George Debenham, Angus and Harry were having coffees and pastries.

Agatha introduced Charles. Olivia beamed. "How nice to meet you," she fluted. "We're practically neighbours."

Charles removed his panama and sat down after placing a chair at the table for Agatha. He smiled pleasantly at Trevor.

"Why did you threaten to kill Aggie?" he asked.

Olivia stared at Charles, her rather rabbity mouth falling open in surprise.

"Who's Aggie?" demanded Trevor sullenly.

"Mrs. Raisin, Agatha. You seem to think she's poking her nose into the investigation into your wife's murder. When I saw you in the cloisters, you were shaking her and threatening her."

All eyes turned to Trevor.

"I didn't know what I was saying," he mumbled. "I'd already had a bit to drink and it was so hopeless. Sorry."

"Most *off* behaviour," said Charles severely. "What if Aggie here had howled for the police, which she had every right to do? They'd have had you off to Nicosia in irons. Are you sure that's all it was—grief and drink? Not frightened of our Aggie finding out who did it?"

Trevor jumped to his feet, knocking his chair backwards with a crash. "Leave me alone," he shouted. He strode to the door, but stopped and turned and said in a quieter voice, "I'll wait for the rest of you in the car. I've had enough of this."

Olivia put a hand on Charles's arm. "You must make allowances for poor Trevor," she said. "We're doing the best we can for him, but he misses Rose dreadfully, and I think it's unhinged him."

90

"But why accuse me of investigating the murder?" asked Agatha. "I'm not," she lied.

"Oh, you told us all those stories when we first met about your investigations," said George. "Didn't she, Harry?"

Harry nodded and Angus said in his usual heavy manner, "Aye, we was talking about it the other night and Olivia here, she says to Trevor, she says, 'I hope our Miss Marple isn't getting in the way o' the police investigation. She might put them on the wrong track althegether, her being an amateur, so to speak.' "

"Well, thanks a lot, Olivia," said Agatha bitterly. "That's what must have set him off."

"It's not all my fault," said Olivia. "You added your bit, too, Angus. You said that the police would be so anxious to find someone, anyone, they could pin this on and get the press off their backs that they would take any daft suggestions from Agatha as gospel. And Harry, you said that it was only in books that amateur detectives were any help. You said in real life they were just people who waited until the police solved the murder and then claimed the credit." She turned on her husband. "And darling, it was you who said to Trevor that someone should drop a quiet word in Agatha's ear."

"I *am* good at investigating," said Agatha furiously. "If you don't believe me, you've only got to ask the police at Mircester. Or ask James!"

Olivia gave a brittle laugh. "If you remember, dear, it was your James who suggested you just blundered about."

"For your information," said Charles, "Aggie is not investigating anything. And why should she? You are such a poisonous, dreary lot of people. Come along, Aggie."

Outside the café, Agatha strode angrily away until they reached the car-park. Then she turned on Charles. "How could you? How could you insult them like that?"

"Come on, Aggie. They'd all just insulted you."

"But don't you see, I don't want to make enemies of

them! I've got to get close to them. Find out what makes them tick."

"Why bother? Does it really matter who killed Rose?"

"Yes, it does!" said Agatha passionately. "It matters desperately who takes the life of another human being. They can't be allowed to get away with it."

"Suit yourself. But if you're going to eat humble pie to that lot, do it on your own. I want lunch. We'll go back to Kyrenia and find somewhere."

"I'm going back to James. I said I would be back at lunch-time, or rather, he said he would be back at lunch-time."

"Waste of space, Aggie," remarked Charles. "He won't care if you don't turn up."

"I shall find out who murdered Rose if it's the last thing I do," shouted Agatha.

"Oh, get in the car."

Agatha took a step towards the passenger side. A rock sailed past her head and struck the rear window of the car, leaving a great jagged hole in the middle of the cracked and starred glass.

Charles, who had been unlocking the car door, stared at Agatha, white-faced.

Then he ran to the entrance to the car-park and looked wildly around. Groups of tourists laden with cameras wandered up and down the narrow streets. Agatha joined him.

"Let's go back and see if they left that café."

At the café, they were told that "their friends" had left a few minutes ago, got into their cars and driven off.

"It could have been kids," said Charles as they emerged again. "But you'd better tell the police and then get the next plane out to England."

"You forget. I'm a suspect, too. I've been told not to leave the island."

"Well, I'll need to report it anyway and get another car."

They went into the Tree of Idleness and Charles asked

92

the manager to call the police. Not only did the police arrive, but several detectives, and the road outside the Tree of Idleness was blocked by police vehicles with flashing blue lights.

Charles made his statement, which was duly recorded. They were told they would be contacted further. Police were fanning out to question tourists and locals if they had seen anything. It all took some time and so, when they finally drove back to Kyrenia and waited for Charles to get another rented car, Agatha realized she was shaken and very hungry. They went to Niazi's, a restaurant famed for its kebabs and slow service, and ate a leisurely meal while Agatha went over and over it all again, debating that if the rock had been thrown at her deliberately, then it must be one of the English suspects.

Charles took himself off to the toilet as soon as the bill arrived. Agatha wondered whether to wait until he returned to see if he would pay it, but decided his sudden departure for the toilet was because he meant her to pay. And, indeed, on his return to the table he thanked her courteously for her "invitation to lunch," said he would see her around, and drifted off.

Agatha drove back to the villa, feeling as she approached it like a guilty and adulterous wife—which was ridiculous, she told herself angrily.

She saw with a sinking heart that not only was James's car outside the villa, but the long, low, official black one used by Pamir.

Agatha was suddenly very tired and upset. Her legs shook and her eyes filled with weak tears. She felt she had endured enough for one day.

James and Pamir were in the kitchen.

"What the hell have you been up to?" demanded James.

"Sit down, Mrs. Raisin," said Pamir. "You have had an upsetting morning. It could have been children. A lot of the local children are very spoilt these days, just like in England. Videos and computers and no discipline. Perhaps some tea for Mrs. Raisin?"

James grumbled something under his breath but got up and switched on the kettle.

"Now, Mrs. Raisin," said Pamir in a more gentle voice than he usually used, "perhaps you might begin at the beginning . . . ?"

"I'm beginning to think if I ever hear those words again, I'll weep," said Agatha.

But she told him everything, about Trevor's threats, which seemed to have been caused by the others' frightening him into thinking that her investigations might cause the wrong suspect to be arrested, and then about the rock thrown at her.

James put a cup of tea in front of her and sat down again.

"And where does Sir Charles come into all this?" asked Pamir. "He was on the island at the time of the murder. I think I should ask him what he was doing."

"Oh, for heaven's sake," snapped Agatha. "He couldn't possibly have anything to do with it. He didn't know any of them."

"Nonetheless . . ."

"Nor is he magician enough to stand outside the car-park when he was already inside it and throw a rock at me."

"Besides," jeered James, "he's a baronet, so he couldn't possibly do anything wrong, could he, dearest?"

Pamir's black fathomless eyes flicked from one angry face to the other.

"Ah, jealousy," he said. "What were you doing, Mr. Lacey, when all this was going on?"

"I was in Nicosia," said James curtly.

"Doing what?"

James flashed Agatha a warning look. "Shopping."

"Where? Which shops?"

"I haven't any warm clothes with me and so I bought a couple of sweaters. I'll probably still be here when the cold weather sets in."

"Let me see."

James went over to the kitchen counter and came back

with a plastic bag. "You will find two sweaters in it and the receipt showing they were purchased today."

"And that was all you did?"

"I went to the Mevlevi Tekke Museum near the Kyrenia Gate, had a look around and then came back here. I came back two hours before you arrived."

Pamir turned and questioned Agatha again, taking her through her whole story, making various notes. Then at last he stood up.

"I would advise you to be careful, Mrs. Raisin. It would be as well if you kept away from the other suspects until this murder is solved."

"I can't be a suspect," said Agatha. "Someone's been trying to kill me."

"Ah, if I were a cynical man, which I am not, I might say there is no evidence of that, only your word."

"But the rock!"

"As I say, that could have been children. I will be talking to you soon."

James saw him out. When he returned to the kitchen, Agatha said, "Before you start jeering about baronets: Like I told Pamir, I went to look for the others, heard they'd gone to Bellapais, and took Charles's offer. I'm tired. Right now I want to forget about the whole thing. Maybe you'd better investigate on your own. Charles blew it for me."

"What do you mean?"

"Charles told them I wasn't investigating anything. He called them a dreary, poisonous bunch of people."

James smiled for the first time. "And so they are. I wouldn't let that stop you. For some reason the Debenhams are staying friends with Trevor and Angus when they would, in ordinary circumstances, walk on the other side of the road if they saw them coming. You've only to show up and smile and apologize for Charles's outburst and they'll be all over you like a rash. Why didn't you come back earlier?"

"I was shaken and hungry and I decided to take up

Charles's offer of lunch, only he turned it into my offer by skating off to the toilet when the bill arrived. He's a cheap-skate."

James smiled again. "You'll know to keep clear of him in future."

"So what did you really get up to in Nicosia?"

"That's my business. I don't want you interfering in it."

"All I've heard today is 'stop interfering,' " said Agatha. "I'm going to have a bath."

"There's water," said James, "and when you've had it, have a rest and then we'll go and make friends with our suspects."

"Are we going to confront Trevor with the fact we know he inherits—or probably inherits—Rose's money?"

"Not yet. No point in driving them away from us. We'll go along and charm them later."

Agatha lay in the bath and stared up at the louvered window above it through which came the roaring sound of the Mediterranean. The events of the day remembered seemed small and bright and not quite real, as if they were all something she had seen in a film.

She was suddenly engulfed in a wave of homesickness. In Carsely she would have had her support group of friends: Mrs. Bloxby, Bill Wong and the members of the Carsely Ladies Society. The trees would be beginning to turn red and gold and the roads around the village would be full of pheasants who seemed well aware that the shooting season had not yet begun. She missed her cats. She hoped Doris Simpson was looking after them properly.

Above all, she wanted to get away from James. The therapy-speakers would ask, "Why are you letting someone live rent-free in your head?" Well, the plain answer to that was that she still liked the lodger. She thought briefly of Charles and then her mind winced away from him.

She climbed out of the deep bath and dried herself. In the bedroom, she switched on the radio in her room, which was tuned to a local English-speaking station which played records. Then the remorselessly bright DJ, a woman with a nasal Essex voice, sang along with the records in a flat monotone, and the records were mostly rap. But as Agatha reached out to switch it off, the music died away and an interview with some member of the north Cyprus National Trust was announced. Agatha decided to listen while she chose something glamorous for the evening ahead. She picked up a little black dress and held it against her. Black could be very ageing. A well-modulated English voice on the radio was talking about snakes, explaining that the poisonous snakes were in the mountains and the harmless snakes at the coast. "But," went on the voice, "the other day I found one of those harmless snakes in my kitchen sink in Kyrenia. I decided just to leave it and after some time it emerged with a rat in its mouth, which all goes to show you what useful creatures snakes are."

Lady, I wouldn't even have a cup of tea in your kitchen, thought Agatha with a shudder.

She tried on the black dress. It was a simple sheath and short enough to show plenty of leg. Perhaps some gold jewellery to brighten it up? Agatha sat down and carefully made up her face in her "fright" mirror, one of those magnifying ones which showed every pore. Then she walked through the bathroom and into James's room where there was a long mirror. Her make-up looked like a thick beige mask and the dress was a mistake. She went into the bathroom and scrubbed off her make-up. Time to start again.

It was only when James shouted up the stairs, "Agatha, are you ready?" that Agatha at last made up her mind what to wear. She put on a white satin blouse and a black pleated skirt, high heels and restrained make-up, and hung some gold chains round her neck. Not exciting, but all she could think of in the final rush.

"I think we should take both cars," she said when she joined James, who was waiting impatiently.

"Why?"

"In case we have to split up for some reason."

"You mean, in case you go off with Charles."

"Don't be so silly."

"It was a practical observation based on events, Agatha."

Agatha felt herself beginning to blush, but she said, "I have no intention of going off with Charles But something may happen—we may become separated."

"I don't want to stand here arguing all night. Take your own bloody car if you want!"

They both left the villa in angry silence and went to their respective cars.

When Agatha got to the end of the road, she saw the petrol gauge was registering empty and so turned right towards Lapta to the nearest garage, instead of left towards Kyrenia. Two huge trucks were blocking the petrol pumps and she had to wait patiently until one of them left. Then she found, because she had taken a smaller bag for evening rather than the large one she usually carried, that she had left all her money back at the villa. She explained, apologized and hurried back to find some money. Then, when she got back to the garage, the proprietor was on the phone and so she had to wait again until he had finished his call. She paid and set out on the road to Kyrenia.

Somehow the homesickness she had felt earlier would not leave her. She longed to be driving down the winding country lanes that led to Carsely, to her thatched cottage, to all the comforts of home. She was almost beginning to dislike James, and yet somehow that craving for love from him would not go away. She hit the steering wheel angrily with her hand. "I wish he would *die*," she said out loud.

She parked on the pavement outside a house. A man opened his front door and stared at her car, which was blocking it.

"I'm sorry," said Agatha, who had just got out. "I'll move it."

The man smiled, showing gold teeth. "No problem," he said cheerfully.

How easygoing they were, marvelled Agatha. If someone drove up on the pavement and blocked my gateway back home, I'd give them a mouthful and call the police.

Bert Mort, the Israeli business man, was just checking out of the hotel when Agatha arrived. He threw her a guilty look.

"Where is your wife?" asked Agatha sweetly.

"Gone back home ahead of me. Look, Agatha, I'm truly sorry."

Agatha relented. "What puzzles me, Bert, is how you could even look at an old bag like me with such a gorgeous wife."

He gave a rueful smile. "Don't put yourself down, Agatha. You've got great legs."

"Agatha!" James stood there, glowering.

"Coming," said Agatha meekly. "Goodbye, Bert. Safe journey."

"They're in the bar," said James. "I thought we should approach them together."

They walked through the lounge and towards the bar. "I feel nervous," said Agatha.

"Just think of your great legs and you'll feel better," said James acidly.

Agatha bit back an angry reply, for they had now reached the entrance to the bar.

Olivia gave them a bleak look, Trevor looked surly and angry, and George Debenham put a protective arm around his wife's shoulders as if to guard her from attack.

"I'm right surprised to see you here," said Angus accusingly and Harry nodded in agreement.

"I owe you all an apology," said Agatha humbly. "I was upset and Charles had heard you having a go at me, Trevor,

99

and he was angry. But I don't know Charles very well and I am not responsible for his remarks. I wouldn't hurt any of you for the world."

"It's all right, Agatha," said Olivia with a sudden warm smile. "We're all rattled by this business and they are still holding the body and poor old Trevor can't get on with the funeral arrangements."

"Sit down and join us," said George "Drink?"

That was easy, almost too easy, thought Agatha, but glad that her apology was over, she ordered a gin and tonic; James ordered a brandy sour.

"The reason we came looking for you," said James, "was that Agatha wanted to take you all out for dinner."

Agatha nearly cried out, "I did?" but bit the exclamation back just in time.

Instead she said, "Where would you like to go?"

"You suggest somewhere," said Olivia.

"There's a very good fish restaurant next to where we are living," said James. "The Altinkaya."

"The manager there is a friend of Jackie and Bilal, the couple who look after us," said Agatha. It sounded like a good idea. The farther they were from Kyrenia, the less chance she had of running into Charles, for she did not want to see the unnerving and cheapskate Charles again.

Agatha was grateful that James did not suggest driving them there; she liked the independence of having her own car and the temporary freedom it gave her from all of them.

James said he would drive off first and all they had to do was follow him.

Agatha walked up the side street to her car. The others had all managed to find parking places opposite the hotel.

As she was opening the door to her car, a familiar voice said in her ear, "Hullo, Aggie."

"Hullo, Charles," said Agatha without turning round.

"Where are you off to?"

"Mind your own business," snapped Agatha, turning around.

"Now what have I done?" he said, looking hurt and bewildered.

"I'll be honest with you, Charles. I don't like tightwads. I don't like fellows who invite me to lunch and then pull that old trick of going to the toilet and leaving me to pay the bill."

He looked pained. "Did I do that? Am I to be blamed for a weak bladder? I thought you invited me, this being the twentieth century."

"No, you invited me."

"Oh, well, that's easily repaired. I haven't eaten. I'll take you for dinner."

"Can't. I'm going to join my friends."

He looked amused. "Not Olivia et al."

"Yes."

"No wonder someone keeps trying to bump you off, Aggie. You don't know when to give up."

"I didn't give up on you."

"No, that's true. I owe you my life, Aggie."

"Okay, I'd best get on," said Agatha, already dreading imagined demands from James as to what had kept her.

He leaned against the car so that she could not get into it. "They were quarrelling this evening in the bar."

"When?"

"I was there about an hour ago and they were all going at it hammer and tongs."

"What about? Could you hear?"

"Trevor was accusing George of having made a pass at Rose. Olivia screamed at Trevor that he was drunk. Angus shouted that Rose was a saint and wouldn't have made a pass at anyone. Harry says, 'Well, she was a bit of a slut.' Trevor tried to punch him. People stare. Waiters come running up. George suddenly mutters something and they all calm down. George offers drinks all round. Olivia coos something at Trevor, Trevor appears to apologize. End of drama."

"Gosh, I wish I'd been there."

"Anyway, Aggie, why don't you just leave it to the police? Someone's trying to bump you off and it must be one of them."

"Mrs. Raisin?"

They both turned. Pamir was walking up the hill towards them. "I have been looking for you," he said. "We found out who threw a rock at your car."

"My car," said Charles.

"The parents brought the boy in. Very bad child from Bellapais. His friends bet him he wouldn't smash the window of a tourist car, so he did. Then he bragged about it."

"Thank you for telling me," said Agatha.

"Most unusual," said Pamir, shaking his head. "We've never had a case like this before. But the boy is, I think, retarded."

"How did you find me?" asked Agatha.

"I phoned your house. You weren't there. I asked at the hotel. You had just left. I looked up this street and saw you here."

"And what about the attack on me at Hilarion?"

"We are still looking into that."

"Where were the Debenhams and the others at the time someone was trying to push me to my death?"

"Mrs. Debenham was lying down in her hotel room, as was Mr. Trevor Wilcox. But we have no proof of that. Angus King and Harry Templeton were both out walking. They say they did not go into any shops, and with so many tourists about, we cannot find anyone to confirm their story. Mr. George Debenham was also out walking. The only person who was definitely up at Saint Hilarion was Mr. Lacey." His dark eyes glittered oddly in the light from the street lamp overhead. "Do you think Mr. Lacey has any reason to be jealous?" His eyes flickered to Charles.

"No reason at all," said Agatha firmly.

"We'll see. Enjoy your evening. A report of the arrest has

been giving to Atlantic Cars, Mr. Fraith." He moved away, his tubby shadow bobbing before him.

"Charles, do move away from the car," said Agatha urgently. "I've got to go."

"So James is a suspect," said Charles, sounding amused. "If you want another refuge for the night, don't hesitate to call on me, Aggie."

He had moved away. Agatha nipped into the car and drove away with an angry roar.

James and the rest were at a large table. Agatha saw Jackie and Bilal at another table by the window and went first to talk to them.

"Is everything all right with the villa?" asked Jackie. "If you want anything, you only have to phone."

"Thank you," said Agatha. They looked such a cheerful, such a *sane* couple, that she was almost tempted to join them and forget about the others. But she smiled and went over to where James was holding a chair out for her.

"What kept you?" he demanded.

"Pamir found out who shied that rock."

"Who?"

"Some kid. He's been bragging about it, his parents heard and brought him in."

"It just shows you," said Olivia, "that the police have been wasting time looking in the wrong direction. It was probably one of the locals who tried to push you out of that window, Agatha, and yet we are plagued with police asking us to account for our movements."

"Hardly likely to be a local," said James. "They like tourists here, particularly the British, though having met some of them, God knows why. And there's such a lot of British expats living here and more coming every year. The Turkish Cypriots are so busy blaming the mainland Turkish settlers for everything that they might wake up one morning to find they are outnumbered by elderly creaking old Brits on retirement pensions."

"But surely the Turks are responsible for all the drugs in north Cyprus?" commented George.

"The Turkish mafia, yes," said James, and added harshly, "with the help of a few Turkish Cypriots who have gone to the bad."

Agatha wondered what he had done in Nicosia and what he had found out.

The manager, Ümit, came up with menus. They all ordered various types of local fish. Waiters arrived with the meze, plates and plates of a bewildering array of delicacies. Bottles of wine were ordered by George. Agatha was amazed again at their capacity for alcohol, for, going by Charles's account, they had all been drinking long before she and James had arrived in the bar at The Dome.

Agatha turned to Angus, who was on the other side of her from James. "How did you meet Rose and Trevor?" she asked.

"It was in London," he said. "I'd just decided to sell up ma businesses and retire and take a wee trip. I'd never been south afore. I saw all the sights, you ken, Buckingham Palace, the Tower, all that stuff. But I got to feeling a wee bittie lonely. I was staying at the Hilton in Park Lane. I was in the bar three nights after I'd arrived in London.

"I saw Rose and Trevor over in the corner. I'd never been much of a ladies' man but I couldnae take ma eyes off her. She was wearing a slinky sort of dress, but it was that laugh of hers and she kept looking over at me, as if inviting me to share the joke. I'd had a wee bit to drink, so I did what I'd never done in ma life afore. I called over the waiter and told him to give them a bottle o' champagne. The next thing was they joined me.

"Well, it was friends from then on. For the rest of ma stay they took me round the pubs and clubs and I'd never had such a good time in ma life. So Rose says, 'Why are you stuck up there in Glasgow? You should be down in Essex with us.' Trevor said he could find me a wee place near to them and so

I moved south. Now Rose is gone, and ah'm telling you this, Agatha, ma life is just one desert."

A tear rolled down his old cheek.

"Why did you never marry?" asked Agatha.

"I came from poor people. I was very ambitious. I got a wee shop after working in the shipyards and saving every penny. It was just a shop selling sweeties and newspapers and things like that. But I made it work and saved everything until I was able to buy another, and then another. I 'member when I got ma first big shop right in the middle o' Glasgow . . . I didnae have any time for romancing, and by the time I did, I was too shy to romance the ladies."

"Sometimes your accent is very broad and sometimes almost English," said Agatha.

"Oh, that was Rose. She said no one south could understand me and sent me to elocution lessons."

"Didn't think of taking any herself?"

"Rose had a beautiful voice," said Angus, looking at Agatha in surprise.

Love is blind, thought Agatha, and deaf as well.

"What are you two talking about?" called Olivia.

"Rose," said Agatha. "I was asking Angus how he had first met Rose and Trevor."

"And did you tell her what great friends we all became?" demanded Trevor, seeming to rouse himself from the alcoholic stupor into which he had suddenly sunk.

"Yes, I was remembering how we had first met at the Hilton," said Angus.

"That was Rose all right," said Trevor. " 'Looks like a fat cat,' " she said.

"I don't understand," said Angus heavily.

"No? Well, my lovely Rose was the most mercenary bitch on God's earth," said Trevor viciously. "She liked money, so long as she never had to go out and earn it, but when it came to handing over any, she was tight-fisted. 'Ask Angus,' she kept saying. 'He's loaded.' So I asked you, didn't I, Angus?

105

And you said"—here Trevor produced a terrible parody of Angus's Scottish voice—" 'Ah've worked all ma life, laddie, and stood on ma ain two feet and Rose will agree wi' me that you should dae the same.' "

"But if Rose had any money, then you'll inherit it," said Agatha bluntly, and James kicked her furiously under the table.

Trevor thrust his face forwards across the table, half-rising, one hand pressing into a dish of olives. "Are you saying I killed my wife to get her money?" he shouted.

"No," said Agatha. "Not at all. Please sit down, Trevor. It was a clumsy remark."

Olivia stood up and went to Trevor. "There now," she said. "No one could ever say our Agatha had any tact. Forget it, do. Have a drink."

Trevor subsided. "I want to go home," he said. "I feel I'll never get home again."

There was a long silence. Agatha could feel James's eyes boring into the side of her face.

"Now, isn't this food delicious?" cried Olivia brightly. "James, you said you were writing a military history. How's it going?"

"Very slowly," said James. "I sit down at the laptop and get out my research notes and then something will happen— the phone will ring, or I'll decide I heard an odd noise in the kitchen that needs investigating, and by the time I return to the computer I don't feel like doing anything."

"Then why bother?" asked George. "You're retired, aren't you? Why not just say to yourself, 'I'm never going to do this'?"

"Oh, I'll get there in the end," said James. "I don't like to give up on anything."

"Neither does Agatha," said Olivia. "She pursued you here."

"Can we change the subject?" said James frostily. "Here's the fish."

Agatha wanted to say something rude to Olivia but felt she was in such deep disgrace already that she was frightened to open her mouth. She suddenly remembered a married colleague in the public-relations business telling her that she dreaded going out on social occasions with her husband because of the post-mortem afterwards: "Why did you say that?" "Did you see so-and-so's face when you said that?" "Couldn't you have found something better to wear? God knows you spend enough on clothes." And man-less Agatha had replied cheerfully, "Why don't you stand up to him? Why don't you tell him to go and get stuffed?"

And now here she was dreading the moment she would be alone with James and listening to his recriminations. The trouble was that she, Agatha, had been brought up in the pre-feminist years, in the "yes, dear" generation. And now that she had a man in her life, all the old patterns had re-emerged. Also men were born with an enviable ability to make women feel guilty about the smallest things, although, she admitted to herself drearily, that telling a man whose wife has just been murdered that her will should see him all right had been a crazy thing to do.

She asked George many questions about his life in the Foreign Office, hoping to repair the damage by being as pleasant and social as she could. George, it transpired, had been desk-bound in London, no glamorous foreign assignments. But he talked and talked. He seemed to miss his old life and his stories were all about more charismatic characters than he was himself. There is nothing quite so boring as listening to someone happily reminiscing about people one has never met, but it had the advantage of taking up most of the evening and deflecting everyone's mind from Trevor's outburst.

At the end of the meal Olivia suggested they should all have coffees and brandies at The Dome. Agatha still did not want to be alone with James, and so she said that was a good idea.

She bolted for her car before James could get to her and

drove off, fumbling in her handbag for her cigarettes. She no longer liked to smoke in front of James because he flapped his hands and coughed angrily.

She drove slowly along the coast road. By the time she got to the hotel, she decided it would be better to take James aside and get the row over with. Otherwise it would be hanging over her for the rest of the evening.

She found James waiting for her by the reception desk. "Before you start," said Agatha, "I've an interesting bit of news. Before we arrived in the bar this evening, that lot were having a terrible row. Trevor accused George of having made a pass at Rose and Harry called Rose a slut and Trevor tried to punch him."

His eyes narrowed. "How did you find that out?"

"Charles told me," said Agatha, and then wished she had said a waiter had told her.

"So that's what kept you," said James furiously. "Let me tell you this, Agatha: This is a small, gossipy place, and you are the one who's getting the reputation as slut."

"That's unfair. He came up to speak to me when I was getting in my car and then Pamir arrived and that's what kept me."

"I don't believe you," shouted James. "And what about your behaviour this evening? We were going to approach the subject of Rose's money *tactfully,* remember? But oh no, you just blurt it out. Damn it, Agatha," he roared. "I could *kill* you."

A girl and a man behind the reception desk froze and stared at both of them, as did several tourists.

James muttered something and turned on his heel and headed for the bar.

Agatha stood for a moment, numb. And then she began to feel very angry indeed. How dare James go on as if he owned her? Why was all his passion confined to bad temper? Well, she was not going back to the villa tonight. She would take a room here and enjoy some peace and quiet.

She fished in her handbag for her credit cards and

108

booked a room for the night. Then, feeling as if she had at last asserted her independence, she walked along to the bar. There was a silence when she joined the others and she had an uncomfortable feeling that they had been discussing her.

She sat down next to Harry on the opposite side of the table from James, avoiding his eyes.

Agatha asked for coffee but refused brandy, saying she had drunk enough.

"Oh, come one, Agatha," urged Olivia. "The night is young, even if we aren't."

"Speak for yourself," said Agatha. "But I am tired of rotting what brain cells I have left with booze."

"That's put a damper on things," said Harry.

Agatha waved the waiter over. "I don't want any coffee," she said firmly. "No coffee."

She stood up again. "I'm going to bed. I want a nice comfortable hotel room, so I've booked in here for the night." And before anyone could say anything, she walked off.

James's remarks were beginning to hurt and hurt badly, so badly she had a mad idea that she might have bruises on her stomach. She hesitated a moment, wondering whether to go back to the villa to get her night-gown and toothbrush and a change of clothes, but suddenly wanted the oblivion of sleep.

She collected her key from the desk. "Staying here, Aggie?"

Charles again.

"I want a quiet night," said Agatha.

"Fallen out with James?"

"Mind your own business."

He got his own key and followed her to the lift. "Come for a drink."

"No," said Agatha firmly. "I am going to sleep."

"I can lend you a pair of pyjamas. We're on the same floor," he said, squinting at the number on her key tag. "And I've got a spare toothbrush, never touched before by the human mouth, still in its pristine wrappings."

"That's kind of you," said Agatha gruffly. "But I'm not sleeping with you."

"Did I ask you?" he said mildly.

In his room, he took out the pyjamas Agatha had worn before, freshly cleaned and ironed by the hotel laundry, and a toothbrush.

"Drink?" he offered.

"Oh, why not?" said Agatha. "I've had so much already but I still feel wide awake. May I smoke?"

"Of course. I smoke occasionally myself. I'll have one of yours."

They sat out on the balcony. Charles leaned back in his chair and looked at the stars twinkling over the sea and did not speak.

Agatha watched him covertly, wondering what made him tick. He was a remarkably clean man, tailored and laundered. Even his neat features and well-brushed hair appeared tailored and laundered. Like a cat, she thought suddenly, neat and self-sufficient.

At last she finished her drink and stood up. "Thanks for the silence, Charles. I really mean it."

"I can be silent any time you like, Aggie. See you around."

And so she left, half-amused, half-puzzled that he could be so casual, so unembarrassed.

At the reception desk, James asked, "Which room is Mrs. Raisin in?" The receptionist told James. "Can you phone her for me?"

The receptionist phoned and then said, "There is no reply, sir, but Mrs. Raisin went upstairs with Sir Charles Fraith. Would you like me to try his room for you?"

"No," said James furiously. "Damn her."

Agatha curled up in her hotel bed and thought about James. She desperately did not want him to be angry with her. He

110

surely must be jealous of Charles. But how could the man be so jealous and be living with her and yet not make any move to make love to her?

She suddenly plunged down into a deep sleep. The night was warm but pleasant and she had not switched on the air-conditioning but had left the windows and shutters open.

At around three in the morning, the lock on her bedroom door clicked softly open. Agatha slept on. A dark figure moved softly towards the bed. With one swift movement, the pillow was snatched from under Agatha's head and pressed down on her face.

Agatha awoke instantly and began to fight for her life. She thrashed and fought and then suddenly, with a wrench of her head, found her mouth free and screamed and screamed. She heard her door slam.

She switched on the bedside light, phoned reception and babbled for help.

An hour later, feeling sick and shivering despite the warmth of the room, she faced Pamir.

She tried to protest that she had told her story to the hotel manager, to various policemen and detectives, but he took her through it again.

When she had finished, he said, "We have taken Mr. Lacey in for questioning."

"What?" said Agatha dizzily. "What has James got to do with it?"

"Mr. Lacey was heard earlier this evening threatening your life. He subsequently tried to call your room and when you were not there, the receptionist volunteered the information that you had gone upstairs with Sir Charles Fraith and might be in his room and volunteered to phone that number, but Mr. Lacey went off in a temper. We must not be side-tracked by the unsolved murder of Rose Wilcox. We think that Mr. Lacey, overcome with jealousy, may have tried to murder you."

"I was able to fight off my attacker," said Agatha. "If James had tried to murder me, I wouldn't have been able to fight him off."

"He may have changed his mind at the last moment."

"Oh, this is rubbish."

"We think this is jealousy. Sir Charles is being questioned also. You are, I believe, wearing Sir Charles's pyjamas." Agatha blushed. She had been too shaken to change, to do anything more but sit on the edge of the bed and shiver.

"I told you. I had a drink with him. That's all. He kindly lent me the pyjamas. How did whoever get the key to my room?"

"Someone may have stolen a passkey. We are questioning the staff."

Agatha clutched her hair. "I know James was not responsible. The whole idea is mad."

Pamir questioned her further and then said she was free to leave. Agatha miserably washed and dressed. She bundled up Charles's pyjamas and put the toothbrush in her handbag and then made her way downstairs and out of the hotel.

She drove back to the villa and let herself in. She felt she should really go to police headquarters and see if she could help James, but she felt too tired and shaken. She went up to her room and lay on the bed. Now every sound seemed sinister. Voices carried up from the beach. People chatting on the road outside sounded as if they were downstairs in the house.

She awoke two hours later with a start. Someone was inside the house. Someone was coming up the stairs.

Agatha was just looking wildly around for a weapon when her bedroom door opened and James came in.

"Oh, James," said Agatha, flooded with gladness. "They let you go!"

He stood in the doorway. "They had no real excuse to keep me. The neighbours were questioned and two of them, returning from a casino at the time I was supposed to be trying to murder you, said they had seen my rented car parked outside the house and had seen me walking in the garden, which is fortunately what I was doing since I could not sleep."

"James, who do you think tried to murder me?"

"Right at this moment, I feel too tired to care. It came out during the interviewing that you had sex with Charles."

Agatha turned dark-red. "That man is no gentleman."

"On the contrary. He lied gallantly, but unfortunately for you, the proof of your love-making was there on the sheets and the hotel staff bore witness to that. They had hitherto kept this interesting fact from me, because I think they were sorry for me. No, Agatha, don't say anything more. You lied to me, as you lied to me about the existence of your husband."

He went out and closed the door.

SIX

†

AGATHA went for a long walk along the beach. There were fewer tourists, and flocks of migrating birds sailed over the cloudless sky overhead.

She was beginning to become angry over her own fear of James and his recriminations. How had it happened that she, Agatha Raisin, once the terror of the public-relations world, should dread another confrontation? Being in love seemed to have sapped her strength. How strange that few people actually talked about love any more. They were obsessed, taken hostage, or co-dependent—anything rather than admit they were not in control, for the very word "love" now meant weakness.

But he was at fault. He was no saint either. He had had affairs even with a woman in the village.

She would need to have it out with him and though she quailed from the idea, she knew she could not go on living under the same roof with him in a hostile atmosphere. As she walked back, the thought that someone was actually trying to

114

kill her made her keep stopping and look warily around. She climbed up the steep hill from the beach to the villa. She felt breathless from the walk and threw away the cigarette she had been smoking. Before smoking had become such a sin, Agatha had thought the whole time about giving up. Now that it was, somehow she could not seem to summon up the will to stop.

She went into the villa. She could hear from the clatter of dishes that James was in the kitchen. She walked in and said to his back, "Come and sit down, James. We can't go on like this. We have to talk."

He turned round, his face hard and closed. But he went and sat at the kitchen table. Agatha pulled out a seat opposite him and sat down.

"I want you to listen to me carefully," began Agatha in an even voice. "You have shown me no love or affection since I came here. I got drunk with Charles and ended up in bed with him. It just happened. I had no reason not to tell you the truth, but I did not want to lose you. But in this loveless whatever-it-is we have between us, you have no right to be angry with me or possessive or jealous. You have hurt me badly. We both want to find out who murdered Rose. But we cannot go on living together like this. What do you suggest?"

He stared at the table in silence.

"James," Agatha pleaded, "I know that any intimate conversation makes you want to shrivel up, but you are going to have to say something."

He looked at her bleakly. "You'll need to give me a little more time, Agatha. I have been behaving badly. In the past I have always had light affairs, nothing very serious. I don't know why it should have to be you. I like very gentle, feminine women. In fact, I feel at ease in the company of rather stupid women. You smoke, you swear, you are dreadfully blunt. If we were married, I think you would drive me mad, Agatha. You are right, I have always shied away from intimacy, not necessarily sex but discussions like this, talking about my feelings. I'll try to watch my temper."

Agatha looked at him sadly. "I don't think I can change, James. I don't think I can turn myself into the type of woman you would like me to be. But I could give up smoking . . ."

He reached forward and took her hand in a warm, firm clasp. "Let's give it a little time. Friends?"

"Friends," echoed Agatha, but feeling in a bewildered way that nothing had been resolved at all. "I'll keep clear of Charles."

"I can't under the circumstances dictate to you who you should see or not see. Now let's discuss our suspects," he said cheerfully, looking, thought Agatha, for all the world like a schoolboy leaving the headmaster's study once a dreaded lecture was over.

"Everything points to Trevor," he said. "And Trevor is drinking like a fish. Sooner or later he is going to betray himself."

"I'm surprised the press haven't been beating at our door after this last attack," said Agatha. "After Olivia's famous press conference, they seem to have disappeared."

"Oh, I forgot to tell you. There's been a dreadful murder over on the Greek side and some British soldiers have been accused. They've all gone over there. Our murder is old hat."

"Well, at least that should give us some peace. Where do we go from here? Back to the hotel this evening?"

"I can't. I've got an appointment in Nicosia this evening."

"I'll come with you."

"No, Agatha, it's got to do with my investigations into Mustafa, and I don't want you involved. Don't go to them on your own. Why not spend a quiet evening here and watch some television?"

"Apart from the local news, there's hardly anything in English."

"Sometimes the local station puts on a film in English."

"All right," said Agatha. "I haven't really had a quiet evening since I've been here."

"I'll go and get ready then," said James, and Agatha was left to her thoughts.

When he had left, she took a cup of coffee out into the garden and watched the sun set until a nasty mosquito bite drove her indoors to look for ointment. Having applied it, she switched on the television and flicked through the channels. All Turkish. Arnold Schwarzenegger shouted in Turkish, Bugs Bunny shouted in Turkish, everyone shouted in Turkish. She switched it off.

Suddenly the villa seemed very quiet and almost sinister. For once, the sea was calm and no children played in the road outside. She began to feel edgy and jumpy.

And then the phone rang. She stared at it, startled, and then, with relief, decided it must be James.

She picked up the receiver.

"Hullo, Aggie."

Charles.

"What do you want?" she demanded, feeling a lurch of disappointment. "And how did you get this number?"

"Easy," he said cheerfully. "You left it with the manager of the hotel. Had dinner?"

"Not yet. But I'm not going to pay for yours."

"Nasty. I was going to pay for yours."

"Charles, I've got into enough trouble over you. James found out I had slept with you."

"That wasn't my fault. They'd found that out from the hotel servants and had tactfully kept that information from James until someone tried to smother you."

"How do you know James isn't here?"

"I was coming back into Kyrenia and he passed me like the clappers, heading off in the direction of Nicosia. Come on, Aggie. Come out to play. I'm bored."

Agatha hesitated, thinking of an evening on her own and jumping nervously at every single sound.

"Oh, all right," she said ungraciously. "Where will I meet you?"

"Here. The Dome."

Agatha sighed. "I should be investigating, but I don't think I want to run into any of that lot this evening."

"What about that restaurant called The Grapevine?"

"No, they might be there. All the British go there."

"What about the Saray Hotel in Nicosia?"

"Well . . ."

"Nicosia's a big place. But if you think James will be there . . ."

"No, come to think of it, if he is where I think he is, he'll be nowhere near the centre. I'll park my car up on the main street, just outside the newspaper shop, and you can drive me from there."

"What's the time? It's only seven. I'll pick you up there at eight."

But Agatha suddenly did not want to wait in the villa longer than she had to. "It'll take me ten minutes to change and about ten minutes to get there," she said. "Make it seven-thirty."

She rang off and ran up the stairs and put on the little black dress she had shunned the night before. After a hasty wash-down, she re-applied her make up, grabbed her handbag and fled the villa.

Glad to be out and free of what she felt was the sinister silence of the villa, she headed for Kyrenia along the now familiar road with the mountains towering up on one side and the sea stretched out on the other. Remembering Kyrenia's irritating one-way system, she went along the ring road to the lights and turned left down into Kyrenia, past The Grapevine, wondering if Olivia and the others were there, past the roundabout and the town hall, and found to her delight that a car was just moving out from a parking place outside the newspaper shop, and slid neatly into the empty space. Charles appeared promptly. She climbed into his rented car.

To avoid going back all around the town, he executed a neat turn under the blaring horn and flashing lights of a Turkish truck and headed back round the roundabout and out towards Nicosia, along past the Onar Village Hotel and up over the mountains until the twinkling lights of Nicosia appeared below them on the plain.

"So how are you feeling?" he asked.

"A bit shaken. Sort of unreal. As if it had all never happened and I'll wake up in my bed in Carsely."

"What sort of place have you got?"

"A thatched cottage, like the kind you see on calendars or biscuit boxes. Little garden at the front and a bigger one at the back. Two bedrooms, bathroom, kitchen, dining-room and living-room. God, I wish I were there."

"I don't think Pamir can keep you here for much longer. Why don't you go and see him tomorrow and tell him you want to go home?"

"There's James."

"Is he still talking to you?"

"Yes."

"Amazing. I wouldn't."

"I don't want to talk about James," said Agatha firmly.

He drove competently into the centre of Nicosia and managed to find a parking place near The Saray.

"What I can't understand about this hotel," said Agatha as they ascended in the lift to the restaurant, "is how they get away with only having two loos next to the restaurant. Only two public toilets for a hotel this size. How do they cope when they have, say, a wedding reception?"

"Don't know. Maybe they piss off the terrace," said Charles indifferently. "Here we are. Do you want a drink at the bar or will we go straight into the restaurant?"

"The restaurant, I think. I've been drinking too much."

"The trouble is booze here is so cheap."

"And cigarettes," said Agatha. "It's a smoker's dream. Everyone smokes, ashtrays everywhere, even in the butcher's."

They ordered their meal and looked out at the lights of Nicosia.

The hors-d'oeuvre was a light flaky pastry filled with cheese, and the main course was lamb on the bone with salad and rice. Charles had ordered a bottle of wine and Agatha forgot her resolution not to drink. It was so easy to talk to Charles. But then she wasn't in love with Charles.

"So who do you think tried to murder you?" Charles asked over coffee and brandies.

"Trevor," said Agatha. "I'm sure it must have been Trevor."

"I would have thought by three in the morning our Trevor would have been deep in an alcoholic stupor. Was there a strong smell of booze?"

"I was too frightened to smell anything. Besides, I had been drinking a lot myself. It's like smoking. If you smoke, then you don't much notice the smell of other people's cigarette smoke."

"Let me think. There's friend Harry Templeton, old but still quite powerful from a lifetime of shifting bales of hay or whatever. Now he said Rose was a slut. He's devoted to Olivia. Could he have thought that George was about to stray and, loyal friend that he is, decided to eliminate the temptress?"

"Far-fetched."

"The whole thing's far-fetched. Apart from various flare-ups at the border between the Greeks and the Turks, this place is the safest in the Mediterranean. There have certainly been a few burglaries of British residents' homes, but the police practically always find the culprits. They've got a big success rate. Only the tourists bother to lock their cars. So the very idea of the murder of a British tourist in a night-club is extraordinary. And yet Trevor is the obvious suspect. He needs money, Rose has money, she won't give him any, his business is down the tubes, and she's a flirt and he's a jealous man. Must be Trevor. And I don't think you're going to have to use your investigative powers on this one, Aggie, because if it's

Trevor, and considering the amount of alcohol he sinks, I think he'll crack. Pamir will keep after us all with his endless questions."

Agatha gave a rueful smile. " 'Could you go through it all from the beginning, Mrs. Raisin?' He has incredible patience."

"He's waiting for one of us to slip up and tell him something different," said Charles. "And he thinks James might have tried to bump you off in a fit of passion."

"James had an alibi."

"I didn't. Lucky James. Pamir implied that people like me suffer from inbreeding in the family and could be potty."

"I sometimes think you're potty myself, Charles. Why bother with me?"

"You amuse me."

"Not very flattering."

"You actually look good in that black dress."

"Thank you. You must be the only man in this hot climate to wear a tie." Charles was wearing a striped silk tie with an impeccable white shirt and a white linen suit. "Don't you ever sweat?"

"Only when I'm making love to you, Aggie."

Agatha sighed. "If only you were the right man. I'm at least ten years older than you, Charles."

"I've always wanted to be a toy-boy."

"And I've never wanted one."

"What about that young Chinese policeman? I thought he was rather keen on you."

"Bill Wong is a friend of mine. In fact, he was my first real friend."

"But he's only in his twenties. You can't have known him long."

"When I worked in London, before I took early retirement," said Agatha, resting her chin on her hands, "I was too ambitious to have friends and I didn't feel the need for any. I built up a successful public-relations business."

"But surely public-relations involves getting on with people?"

Agatha laughed. "In my case, I think I was successful because I bullied and cajoled and threatened. When I moved to the Cotswolds, things changed. I no longer had my work as my identity. I met Bill on what I like to think as my first case. Then there came other friends."

"Life begins at fifty?"

"Something like that. What about you, Charles? No wish to get married?"

"This is so sudden."

"Be serious."

"Never found the right girl. Have no burning desire for children."

"That's sad."

"Then we're a sad pair, Aggie. You haven't got children either."

"No," said Agatha sadly, "and now I never will. Wasted years, Charles."

He ordered another two brandies and raised his glass. "Here's to the wasted years," he said solemnly.

"Are you sure you ought to be driving after drinking this lot?" demanded Agatha.

"They do breathalyse people here just like back home, but I shall drive home carefully. I don't feel in the least bit tipsy."

When they finally rose to leave, Agatha said, "I hope James is back. I don't relish the idea of being in that villa on my own."

His eyes twinkled maliciously. "We could spend the night here."

"Forget it. Let's just go."

As they were driving out of Nicosia towards the Kyrenia Road, Agatha saw they were approaching the Great Eastern Hotel and she started to think about James. What was he up to?

And then, with a lurch of her heart, she saw him walking along the street with a girl on his arm, a girl with long brown curly hair, a short, short skirt and long, long legs. They were going in the direction of the town.

"That was James!" gasped Agatha. "Turn the car."

"You'll need to wait, Aggie, until the next corner. This is a dual carriageway."

Agatha waited impatiently until Charles was able to swing round and head back. And then, in front of them on the deserted street and under the lights of the street lamps, they saw James. His arm was around the girl. Charles slowed to a crawl. James and the girl turned a corner into a side street. Charles parked at the side of the road.

"Out we get," he said cheerfully, "and see where they're going. Unless you want to confront them."

"No," said Agatha hurriedly. "This might be part of his investigations."

"And very nice, too," murmured Charles. "What investigations?"

"He wants to find out if his old fixer who runs a brothel is dealing drugs."

James and his companion turned in at a block of flats in the side street. Charles and Agatha walked along and stood on the other side of the block of flats.

"Now what do we do?" asked Charles.

They gazed up at the block of flats. And then a light came on in one of the windows on the second floor, and like watching people on a stage set, they saw James and the girl.

The girl said something and laughed, and took off her short jacket.

James went up to her, put his arms around her and kissed her, a long, deep embrace. She drew back and began to unbutton her blouse.

James crossed to the window and jerked down the blinds.

Agatha found she was trembling.

"Well, well, well," said Charles. "Who would have thought it. Don't break your heart, Aggie. That was a prostitute if ever I saw one."

"You don't kiss prostitutes like that," said Agatha bleakly.

"We can't stand here all night. Do you want to go up and bang on the door and throw a scene?"

"No," said Agatha, "I just want to go home."

They walked back to the car. When they drove off, Agatha said, "That's that. I don't feel anything for him any more. How could he?"

"Getting even? Maybe the poor man is still wondering how you could sleep with me."

"That was different."

"I suppose it was. You didn't have to pay me."

"Are you sure that was a prostitute, Charles?"

"Pretty sure."

"But she was pretty."

"A lot of them here are. They come from God-awful places like Romania."

There had been girls in the Great Eastern Hotel, but the bar had been very dark and Agatha had not studied any of them very closely.

Perhaps the girl was one of the prostitutes from the Great Eastern Hotel and this was James's way of finding out information about Mustafa. But he could simply have offered her money. There was no need to kiss her like that. Agatha felt beyond tears.

They drove the rest of the way to Kyrenia in silence.

When they reached Agatha's car, Charles said, "Want to come to the hotel for a nightcap?"

Agatha shook her head.

"Good-night kiss?"

"No, I don't feel like it."

"Try not to weep all night into your pillow. You're worth better than James, Aggie."

Agatha got out of the car and waved to Charles as he drove away.

Then she drove back to the villa and let herself in. Grief was being replaced by rage. She paced up and down the living-room, wondering what she should say to him when he returned, wondering whether to say anything at all. He had not laid a finger on her and yet he had kissed that girl so passionately.

She felt lonely, old and unwanted.

Then, with a hardening of the heart, she went upstairs and put her night-gown—froths of satin and lace bought especially to charm James—into a small traveling-bag along with make-up, a change of clothes and a toothbrush. Then she went out, locked up and got back into her car and drove back to Kyrenia.

In the hotel reception a late busload of Israeli tourists had just arrived and were milling around the reception area and so Agatha was able to get into the lift unobserved.

Charles opened his bedroom door in answer to her knock.

"Come in," he said. "We'll have a drink and then you'll take the spare bed, Aggie. I don't want to be made love to by a woman with a mind full of revenge."

"You are very kind, Charles," said Agatha with a break in her voice.

"Not me. You're a laugh a minute, Aggie. We'll have a bottle of wine on the balcony."

"I don't know what my liver's going to be like after all this booze," said Agatha.

"You'll soon be back in Carsely and you can drink herb tea until it comes out your ears."

They sat together on the balcony. "I don't know how to handle this," said Agatha. "I don't know what to do."

"Then do nothing. That's what I would do, Aggie. When in doubt, do nothing. If you tell him you saw him, he might, as you guessed, tell you it was part of his investigations, and then you'll start shouting about the way he kissed that girl, and he'll say he had to make it look good and don't be silly, and you'll have got exactly nowhere. Also we're both assuming naïvely that he means to spend the night. He may even be back at the villa now. So how do you explain your absence?"

"I'll say I was frightened to be on my own and so I took a room here."

"Why don't you jack the whole thing in, Aggie? It's all a mess. Go back to Carsely. Go in for something safe like flower-arranging. Forget about Rose's murder. If Trevor did it, he'll probably eventually confess when he's drunk, and you'll have wasted all this time for nothing."

"I've got to find out," said Agatha. "There has to be some point to all this. It'll keep my mind off James."

"After tonight, my sweet, your mind should be permanently off James."

"I suppose so. Did you see anything of my suspects today?"

"Not a sign. I suppose Pamir will soon be looking for you again. If sheer doggedness and perseverance can find out who murdered Rose, then he'll do it."

"I suppose it's my vanity," said Agatha.

"You mean the reasons you're so hurt by James?"

"No, I mean about solving the murder. James saying I had just blundered about in murder investigations and that's how they got solved, Olivia's jeers."

"If you must, you must. It's late. Let's to bed."

Agatha went into the bathroom, had a shower, and changed into the night-gown.

Charles blinked at her when she emerged. "That night-gown makes me regret I offered you the spare bed. Go to bed, Aggie, before I change my mind."

Agatha climbed into bed. Her head when she laid it on the pillow swam uncomfortably. No more drink, she thought, whatever James gets up to.

She was then aware fifteen minutes later of Charles emerging from the bathroom. She stiffened under the sheets, waiting for some approach. But he got quietly into his own bed and was soon asleep, snoring dreadfully. How could such a neat and self-contained man snore like that, thought Agatha crossly. She wearily got out of bed and seized him by the shoulders and turned him on his side.

Then she got back into her own bed, now wide awake. She stared at the ceiling, thinking of James, trying to eradicate that bright picture of what she had seen through the apartment window in Nicosia. Then she suddenly fell fast asleep, not waking until the next morning at nine o'clock.

Charles was pottering around the room. "You'd best straighten up your bed and hide in the bathroom while I order some breakfast. We'll have it on the balcony."

Memories of the evening before flooded Agatha's weary brain. But she washed and dressed and waited in the bathroom until she heard room service deliver their breakfast and leave.

Agatha sat on the balcony and crumbled a croissant between her fingers. "I've been thinking," she said slowly, "that I'll go to Nicosia after I've been to the villa and ask for permission to go home."

"Good idea."

Agatha stood up. "I don't want any more breakfast. Thanks for dinner and everything, Charles. I'm sorry I called you a cheapskate."

"Wait till you get my bill for services rendered."

Agatha held out her hand. "So this is goodbye."

He solemnly shook her hand.

"See you around the Cotswolds, Aggie."

Agatha drove back to the villa. She felt suddenly calm. She would see what James had to say, see how he would react. She would be dignified. She would not rant or scream.

It was another perfect day with only the lightest of breezes.

She took a deep breath and let herself into the villa and called, "James!"

There was no reply and then she noticed that his laptop and research papers and books, which were usually piled up on the table, had all gone. She ran outside again. His car was not there. Something she had been too pent up to notice when she arrived!

She went back in and up to his bedroom. The wardrobe door was open, showing nothing but empty hangers. And the she saw an envelope with her name on it on the pillow.

She opened it.

"Dear Agatha," she read. "My investigations have taken me off to Turkey for some time. The rent here is paid for another month. I waited for you last night, but you did not come home, so it did not take much imagination to guess where you were. Goodbye. James."

Agatha sat down on the bed and stared around the empty room. How on earth could James go to Turkey? All of them had been told not to leave the island.

She should phone Pamir. In fact, she'd better phone Pamir, for sooner or later he would be round and wondering where James had got to.

She went downstairs. She fished in her handbag for her notebook, where she had written down Pamir's number.

When he came on the phone, she told him about James's going off to Turkey. "Why should he go there?" demanded Pamir sharply.

In for a penny, in for a pound, thought Agatha. "He was annoyed with his old fixer, Mustafa. He wanted to get even with him for having cheated him over the rent of the first villa and so he was out to prove Mustafa was dealing in drugs."

"He should have consulted us," said Pamir. "We already told him Mustafa was being investigated."

"How could he get off the island without your knowing?" asked Agatha.

"Easy. Turkey is only across the water. He could have got a fishing boat or a pleasure boat or a yacht."

"Aren't you going to do anything about it?"

"We will look for him, be assured of that. Be careful not to follow his example, Mrs. Raisin, or we shall be very angry."

"I meant to come and see you anyway," said Agatha. "I would like to go home."

"As would the other suspects. Not yet, Mrs. Raisin."

"When?"

"Soon, I hope."

"If you find out where James is, will you let me know?"

"We will do our best."

And that was that. Trapped in north Cyprus.

The phone rang. Agatha snatched up the receiver.

"James? Where the hell are you?"

"Not James. Charles."

"Oh."

"Are you off?"

"No, I'm not off. James is off. He's disappeared to Turkey. Now what do I do?"

"Well, your suspects are off to Salamis today."

"What's that?"

"It's over near Famagusta. In ancient times, it was one of the leading cities of Cyprus. They're going swimming at Silver Beach first, which is next to it. Want to bring your bathing-suit and observe the murderers at play?"

"May as well. Nothing else to do."

"Pick me up. Your turn to pay for the petrol. And bring a picnic."

"All right. But no wine. I need a dry day."

Agatha went first to the petrol station and then to the super-market beyond. She bought bread, cheese, olives, a tin of salmon, lettuce, tomatoes, green peppers and some cakes and a bottle of local wine. She had already packed a carton with dishes and glasses before leaving the villa. Not a very exciting lunch, she thought, but if Charles doesn't like it, he can buy me lunch.

Charles was waiting outside The Dome. "They left about an hour ago, Aggie, but from the conversation I overheard, they plan to make a day of it."

Once more over the mountains and out on the Famagusta Road. "Give me your guidebook and I'll tell you about Salamis," said Charles as Agatha negotiated a hairpin bend.

"In my handbag."

Charles fished it out. "What a lot of history. Let me see. According to legend, the city was founded by the Homeric hero Teucer when he was exiled by his father, Telemon, king of the Greek island of Salamis, on his return from the Trojan war around 1180 B.C. And so forth. Yawn. By the eighth century it was a major trading centre, became first city in Cyprus to mint its own coinage. Fell to the Persians. Defeated two hundred years later by Alexander the Great. Under siege after his death. Are you taking all this dry stuff in, Aggie? Watch that truck! Glorious place again under the Byzantines. Then shattered by earthquake and tidal wave. City rebuilt, renamed Constantia in honour of Constantius the Second, the reigning Byzantine emperor. Never fully recovered. Harbour silted up. Most of the city under thick cover of sand. Signpost to the place is about five miles north of Famagusta. You can read the rest for yourself. Bring your swim-suit?"

"I've got it on under my dress."

"We'll go for a swim, have our picnic and then look for the others. I don't know if I really want to go trekking around ruins on such a hot day. It says here stout shoes, long socks and some sort of head-covering are strongly recommended. We can park at the site, but I would suggest we park on the beach first and then walk to the site if that's where the others have gone."

* * *

Silver Beach turned out to be a long stretch of gently shelving sand disappearing into the green-blue waters of the Mediterranean.

They undressed and went for a swim. Agatha turned over and floated on her back, feeling the sun warm on her face. The day was perfect. A world away from murder and mayhem. She wondered what Charles really thought of her and why he should bother to spend time with her. The fact was that Agatha had become so demoralized by her chilly relationship with James that she could not imagine any man wanting to spend any time at all in her company.

She rolled over and headed back for the beach, suddenly hungry.

Charles joined her, in swimming-trunks and with not a hair out of place, as she laid out what began to look like a very uninteresting picnic on a cloth on the beach.

"Don't you tan?" asked Agatha, looking at his white, smooth chest.

"I never tan. I don't know why. Thick English skin or something. What goodies do we have? Dear me. I hope you've brought an English can opener for that salmon, Aggie. The Turkish Cypriot ones don't work."

But Agatha had only a local can opener, which ran around the rim of the tin of salmon without piercing it at all.

"There's bread and cheese and things," she said defiantly. "And I got some cakes."

"There's a restaurant there."

"Oh, all right," grumbled Agatha. "I'll pack all this up again and have it for supper."

She then set about performing the tricky business of drying herself and slipping off her swim-suit under her dress and hauling on her knickers over wet and salty thighs. Charles wrapped a large beach towel around his waist and removed his swimming-trunks and put on his underwear and trousers and then a shirt without any of the struggles Agatha was enduring.

131

They put the unwanted picnic and swim-suits in the car and headed for the restaurant.

Charles ordered wine despite Agatha's protests that sooner or later they would be stopped and breathalysed. "Not if we keep within the speed limit," said Charles. "Anyway, we can have a sleep on the beach afterwards."

"You forget why we came," said Agatha. "To go look for the others."

"Later. Let's not spoil the day."

Agatha ate kebab and looked out onto the beach. It was a tranquil scene. The water was crystal-clear. She wondered where they put their sewage. Then a sudden longing for James hit her like a wave. How could he go off, just like that? Had she ever really known him?

"He'll probably turn up in Carsely sooner or later, after playing Lawrence of Arabia or whatever he's doing," said Charles, guessing her thoughts.

"You can't play Lawrence of Arabia in Turkey," said Agatha with a watery smile. "I don't want to eat any more. May I have a cigarette?"

"Of course. And give me one as well."

"Don't you ever buy any for yourself?"

"No, that would mean I would have to admit to myself that I smoke. Besides, smokers are usually all too eager to pass out their fags. Make another addict like themselves."

"I shouldn't give you one."

He leaned forwards and extracted one from her packet and lit it up.

"So we'll order coffee," he said, "and go and find your suspects. Isn't it peculiar the way they all seemed to have worked each other up to the idea that your interference could cause trouble? Maybe one of them wanted you warned off."

"Maybe. I'm frightened someone will have a go at me again. One of them is taking me seriously. James shouldn't have left me to face this alone."

"I'm here."

"True, but . . ."

"I lack gravitas. Bad-tempered people always carry weight."

"James is *not* bad-tempered!"

"If you say so."

Agatha thought of James. She had to admit that he had been bad-tempered since she arrived, but finding yourself in the middle of a murder was enough to make anyone bad-tempered, she thought defensively, to keep the idea at bay that it was her unwelcome pursuit of him that had turned him nasty.

"I suppose you expect me to pay for this," said Agatha.

"Yes, thank you."

"You *are* a cheapskate."

"No, Aggie, I am your twentieth-century man. You wanted equal rights and that means equal expenses. If you stop bitching I'll take you to dinner tonight."

"James might be back."

"Dream on. Now the path from this beach only leads to the old harbour. I had a look at your guidebook. We'd better drive round."

"No sleep?"

"No, I'm awake now."

They drove round to the site and parked outside the old amphitheatre. A bearded guide in a battered sports jacket was just about to take a party around. "I am Ali Ozel," he introduced himself after waving them over. "You may join my tour if you like."

"That's very kind of you," said Charles, "but we're looking for some friends."

"I may have seen them," said Ali. "What do they look like?"

"One woman, middle-aged, scrawny, arrogant, high commanding voice, with four men. One her husband, thin and sallow, quiet; friend Harry, farmer, elderly, thinning white hair; Angus, Scottish and proud of it, looks a bit like Harry; Trevor, fair hair, thick lips, beer belly, ghastly pink from the sun, truculent."

Ali's eyes twinkled with amusement. "You *did* say they were friends of yours? I did see some people like that about an hour ago, but I haven't seen them since."

"Okay, thanks anyway. We'll look for them." Charles took Agatha's arm and led her into the ruins of Salamis.

They ploughed their way through the ruins. Charles was particularly impressed by an open-plan latrine with seating for forty-four people. The ruins were bright with tourists in multi-coloured holiday clothes. The sun was dazzling. Agatha would just think she had seen her quarry, and then the group would turn out to be totally different people.

The tall columns of the gymnasium stood proudly up against the blue sky. Charles appeared to have forgotten why they were at Salamis and enthusiastically took control of Agatha's guidebook, wandering here and there, admiring everything.

There are a great many ruins at Salamis and they cover a wide area. Agatha began to become weary and would have liked to sit down somewhere in the shade and wait for Charles, but she did not want to be alone, not with Olivia and the others possibly somewhere around.

They trudged ever onwards until Charles consulted the guidebook and said he would like to see the tombs of the kings. A map showed them to be situated on the other side of the main Famagusta road. "Better walk back and take the car," said Charles.

They walked back to the car-park and then drove back out to the road and so to the tombs. They bought tickets at a museum which was more of a dusty hut with replicas of a chariot and a hearse. They left the museum and walked towards the tombs.

The nearest tomb has a broad shallow ramp leading to the burial chamber with the skeletons of two horses at the entrance, where the animals were cremated after pulling the king to the burial chamber. The tombs where kings and nobles were buried dated from the seventh and eighth centuries B.C. They were buried along with their horses and chariots, favourite slaves, food, wine and other necessities for the afterlife.

It was when they had got to the fiftieth tomb of the hundred and fifty tombs and just when Agatha thought she could not walk a step farther that Ali Ozel appeared with his tourists.

"I saw your friends," he said.

"Where?" demanded Agatha.

"Back towards the gymnasium. You said five of them, but there were only four, looking for a fifth, who had disappeared."

"We'd better go," said Agatha to Charles, all her energy renewed.

They walked back to the car-park and drove to the gymnasium. There were only a few tourists, but no Olivia, husband or friends. The pillars were beginning to cast long black shadows across the gymnasium.

"Back out to the car-park," said Charles. "We might just catch them."

But at the entrance, before they reached the car-park, they could hear Olivia's voice questioning another guide. "Haven't you see him?"

Agatha and Charles went up to her. Her husband George, Trevor and Angus stood a little way away.

"What's up?" asked Agatha.

Olivia swung round. "We lost Harry."

"Wasn't he with you?"

"Of course he was. But he wandered off towards the beach. You know, there's a Roman villa and then a crossroads with a track leading down to the sea. He said he wanted to see what kind of beach it was. We then all agreed to go different ways to look at different things and then meet up in the gymnasium. When he didn't come back, we went down to the beach but there was no sign of him. We all spread out and began to search and agreed to meet up in the gymnasium again, which we did, but none of us has been able to find Harry, and I'm tired and don't want to be stuck here all day."

"You are the murder people," said the guide suddenly. "I see you on television."

Olivia ignored him, but Agatha saw the guide go into his little office and pick up the phone.

"We'll try the beach again for you," said Charles. "Maybe you missed him."

"But that's miles," groaned Agatha.

"Then you wait here," said Charles. "I'll go alone."

"No, I'm coming with you." Agatha did not want to be left with them in case one of them tried to murder her.

They set off as the sun fell lower in the sky. There were few tourists now. Ali passed them and shouted, "Any luck?" They shook their heads and pressed on until they came to the crossroads."

"It should be easier to search now," said Charles. "Most people will have left the beach."

They almost ran down the narrow road to the beach, Agatha forgetting her fatigue in her desire to find Harry.

The beach was nearly deserted. A yacht bobbed out on the water. The sea was calm, with only little waves rippling in across the sand.

And then, along the beach, they saw a lone figure, lying prone. The top half of the body was mostly covered by a newspaper, its pages rising and falling in the slight breeze.

Charles pointed. "Do you think that's him?"

"May as well go and see." Agatha headed along the beach and Charles followed.

They both stood together at last, looking down.

"Seems to be asleep," said Charles. "Do you think those are Harry's feet?"

"I don't know what Harry's feet look like," said Agatha. "Here goes."

She bent down and gently drew away the newspaper

which was covering the man's face and top half of his body, noting that it was *Kibris,* a Turkish Cypriot paper.

Agatha knew immediately, before she saw the broad red stain on the front of Harry's shirt, that he was dead. The face was as lifeless as clay. Someone had closed his eyes.

All the frights she had endured, the two attempts on her life, the long hot day and now this made Agatha feel sick, and dizzy and faint. She sat down on the sand and put her head between her knees.

"Stay there," said Charles urgently. "I'll get help."

So Agatha sat where she was, beside the dead body of Harry. A woman passed her, leading a small child by the hand. She stopped and turned back and stared open-mouthed at the dead body, at the gruesome red stain on the shirt. Then she scooped up the child and ran off down the beach, screaming at the top of her voice.

Agatha stayed, unmoving. Her mind seemed to be a numb blank. In the distance, she heard the wail of police sirens. She felt very tired.

Then she was dimly aware of being surrounded by people, of Charles's saying sharply, "Can't you see she's in shock? I was with her when we found the body. I'll answer any questions."

He helped Agatha to her feet. She blinked and stared around in a dazed way.

Pamir was there, his face grim. "If you will just step aside for a moment with Sir Charles," he said to Agatha. "Only a few preliminary questions."

With Charles's arm around her waist, Agatha walked up the beach.

"Now we will sit down here," said Pamir. "You first, Sir Charles."

So Charles painstakingly went through their day, ending up with the finding of Harry.

In a dreary little voice, Agatha then told the same story.

"You may go," said Pamir. "I will call on you later."

"I'll be with Mrs. Raisin at the villa," said Charles.

Agatha wanted to cry out that James might be there, but felt too weak and shaky to protest.

Charles said he would drive. She fell asleep on the road back to Kyrenia, awaking only when they stopped outside The Dome.

"Wait there," said Charles. "I'll get my stuff."

He's going to move into the villa, thought Agatha with a stab of panic. She still cherished a hope that James might be there waiting for her.

Bright images of the day crowded her head—the ruins, the ancient brutality of the tombs, Harry's still, dead face and closed eyes facing up to the sun. Who had closed his eyes? The killer, no doubt.

She fumbled in her handbag for a cigarette and lit it. What were they doing in Carsely, sleepy Carsely that she used to despise for its lack of excitement? She thought longingly of the vicarage, where Mrs. Bloxby would produce tea and scones and they would sit by the fire and chat about safe and secure village matters. Would she ever see her home again? Or would the killer, who had tried to get rid of her twice and failed, be successful on the third attempt? She shivered, suddenly glad that she was not going to be alone in the villa. Damn James for a heartless, selfish beast. He should be there to protect her. Yes, he hadn't even thought of that! Two attempts on her life and he had cleared off, leaving her alone. He didn't care a rap for her or he would not have gone. Forget the analysis-paralysis and look at the footwork. She could not possibly imagine that a man who had any feeling for her at all could leave her in such peril.

Charles came out of the hotel, carrying two expensive suitcases which he put in the boot.

He slid in behind the steering wheel.

"You're very kind," volunteered Agatha.

"Think nothing of it," said Charles. "You're saving me a hotel bill."

The rest of the evening went by like a bad dream. Pamir came at eight o'clock to grill both of them again. His anger seemed to have mounted. Outside, the press waited eagerly. The murder on the Greek side was old hat.

At last Pamir left.

"We can't go out anywhere without being plagued by the press," said Charles. "They will keep banging on the door. There they go again."

But a voice shouted, "British High Commission here."

Charles went to let a small, dapper man in, blinking in the sudden blast of flashes from press cameras.

He introduced himself as Mr. Urquhart and advised them, unnecessarily, as Charles acidly pointed out, to co-operate with the police. Then he began to question Agatha closely about James Lacey. Where was he? Turkey? Was she sure? He could still be on the island.

"If he were," said Agatha, "then he certainly would not be at Salamis, murdering poor old Harry Templeton."

"This is all most unfortunate," said Mr. Urquhart. "The police were about to release Mrs. Wilcox's body and let you all go home, but in the light of this latest murder they are certainly not going to let any of you go."

He then questioned Agatha about James again, but Agatha would only repeat that James had said he was going to Turkey. She did not mention anything about his investigations into Mustafa.

At last Mr. Urquhart departed the villa in a fusillade of flashes. From outside the villa came the nasal voice of a television reporter talking to a camera.

"Do you want to go to bed?" asked Charles. "Or shall we eat first?"

"There's nothing much left in the house," said Agatha. "And I don't feel like the picnic stuff. The phone's ringing again. Maybe I should answer it. It might be James."

"And pigs might fly. I'm hungry. Those few little kebabs

at lunch-time didn't go very far. Tell you what. If we go out the back and shin over the garden wall, we'll find ourselves in the fish-restaurant car-park. I fancy some of those nice little red fish like mullet."

"The press will see us."

"They can't, surely." He opened the back door, which was next to a small laundry-room. "Come here, Aggie. All we need to do is sneak round the corner of the building and over the wall. They'll never see us. That great hedge of mimosa screens us."

The idea of being with other people in a crowded restaurant appealed to Agatha.

They went out, gently closing the door behind them, and climbed over the low wall which separated the villa garden from the car-park.

"Now let's just hope none of the press decides to come in for dinner," said Charles. "But I think they'll stand outside the villa for a bit and then go back to The Dome to join the others who are trying to talk to Olivia and George. Who knows? Olivia may give another press conference."

"What we haven't thought about is who on earth would want to bump off Harry?"

"Harry must have found out who did it," said Agatha. "I suppose it will turn out he was murdered in the same way as Rose."

"Probably. And someone must have been desperate. If it was any of the remaining four, then one of them must have been frightened enough to bump off Harry, knowing that now they really would be suspected and hopes of some mad stray Turk losing his head, as in the murder of Rose, just wouldn't be considered any more."

"I've been thinking about George Debenham," said Charles, deboning a small fish with neat and surgical precision. "Why should he flirt with Rose? He doesn't look the type."

"In the information on them I took down from Bill

Wong, it turns out that George suffered heavy losses on the stock exchange. Did I tell you that? And Rose had money."

"But they had just met. I mean, Rose would hardly say, 'Look, I'm rich. Stick with me and I'll see you all right.' "

"She might not have been blunt like that," said Agatha slowly. "But she might have made some jokey reference to being loaded. No, I think Trevor's jealousy and rage are the cause of these murders. You said Trevor wanted to punch Harry because Harry called Rose a slut."

"Do you want to go to the hotel after dinner and see how they're getting on?"

Agatha repressed a shudder. "After we eat, I just want to go to bed. I've never felt like giving up like this before. I have a longing to go home."

"If you've finished, now's the time," said Charles, looking out through the restaurant doors. "The press have arrived. Quickly."

He threw some money on the table. They had been sitting on the terrace and both went over the edge into the scrub below and made their way cautiously around to the car-park, Agatha hoping that the report of the poisonous snakes keeping to the mountains was true.

They gained the villa without being accosted. "First bath for me," said Agatha with a yawn.

"We sharing a bed?"

"No, Charles. I am too old for casual sex."

"Well, if you change your mind, you know where to find me."

Agatha awoke during the night shivering and found a quilt and put it over her. The weather was beginning to change. The long summer was over.

A police car arrived the next morning to take them to police headquarters in Nicosia. Agatha groaned. "What can he possibly ask us that he hasn't asked us already?"

141

"I didn't tell him about Trevor trying to punch Harry," said Charles. "I think I should. I mean, I hardly know that bunch and don't like them."

"I think that's why Pamir keeps on at us," said Agatha wearily. "He gets a little more each time."

Olivia, George, Angus and Trevor were waiting at police headquarters to be interviewed when they arrived. George looked white and strained under his tan; Trevor, stunned; Angus had aged terribly; and Olivia for once was without any social talk or animation.

They looked up dully when Agatha and Charles entered, but did not say anything.

Agatha and Charles sat down and waited. After half an hour of total silence Pamir arrived, nodded to them and went into the inner room. "Like waiting for the doctor," said Charles.

George Debenham was summoned first. The morning dragged on, the bright sunlight outside seeming to mock the grim dreariness within.

Agatha was called last.

"Now, Mrs. Raisin . . ." began Pamir.

"I know, I know," said Agatha wearily. "I've to tell you all over again, starting at the beginning."

"Not yet. Do you, Mrs. Raisin, not think that you might have precipitated this murder?"

"How? Why?"

"I gather from Sir Charles that you went to Salamis for the sole purpose of finding the others and continuing your amateur investigation."

Yes . . . That's true. But I didn't see any of them until after the murder had been committed."

"But they might have seen you."

"So what made that different to all the other days they had seen me?" said Agatha impatiently. "And if it hadn't been for me and Charles, you might not have found the body until the next day and who knows, by that time the murderer might have returned and shoved the body in the sea, forged a note from Harry saying he had left on a fishing boat or something like James, and you would have been none the wiser."

"We have asked everyone who was on the beach and in the ruins yesterday to come forward. Someone might have seen something. So begin at the beginning . . ."

So Agatha did, vivid memories of the heat and the ruins coming back into her mind.

Then she said, "If one of them murdered Harry, he must have sneaked back to the beach when they split up. And when they were supposed to be searching for him why didn't they find him on the beach?"

"They say that after Mr. Templeton went off to the beach, that they arranged to meet in the gymnasium in an hour. Mrs. Debenham went to look at the basilica; Mr. Debenham said he simply wanted to go back to the gymnasium, sit down and rest and wait for the others; Mr. Wilcox said he wanted to be on his own for a bit; and Mr. Angus King went to look at the tombs. All say they searched the beach, but it was still full of tourists and they did not spot Mr. Templeton."

"So it could have been any of them," said Agatha.

Pamir surveyed her and then leaned back in his chair. "Or you, Mrs. Raisin."

"Me? Why? I barely knew them. I didn't know any of them before I came here."

He leaned forward. "How can I put this? At your age, Mrs. Raisin, ladies can go a little unhinged. It seems to me that since you gave up your career, you have had a desire for prominence and attention, which is why you turned to amateur detective investigation. Perhaps not having any more murders to investigate, you decided to make some of your own."

"That's outrageous," spluttered Agatha.

"Perhaps. But murder is outrageous. Your own behaviour has been erratic."

"But someone tried to kill me—twice!"

143

"There are no witnesses to either attempt. We have only your own word for that. You follow James Lacey to Cyprus because everyone seems to know you are romantically interested in him and yet, after moving in with him, you accept a dinner date with an Israeli business man and who knows where that might have led had not his wife turned up, and then you sleep with Sir Charles. I know this is the permissive society. Such behaviour, however, in a middle-aged lady from an English village is most odd."

"How dare you!" panted Agatha.

"I dare because I am very angry. We have a very low crime rate in north Cyprus. Tourists come here because it is still the safest place in the Mediterranean and I am going to accuse all of you of everything and keep you here until these murders are solved. We have respectable British residents here, Mrs. Raisin, who contribute to the cultural life of the island. They cause no trouble. Until your arrival, we have never suffered anything like this."

"You are insulting. You are looking in the wrong direction. What about Trevor Wilcox? His business is on the skids and Rose wouldn't bail him out. He'll be all right now. He probably inherits her money. And what of George Debenham? He's in debt as well."

"How did you find this out, Mrs. Raisin?"

Damn him, thought Agatha. She could not betray Bill Wong.

"They told me," she muttered.

"They just told you!"

"Something like that."

"I do not believe you," said Pamir. "I think somebody in England found out the information for you."

Sweating now, Agatha hoped the manager of The Dome had not told the police about her fax to police headquarters in Mircester. She wanted to run away from this room, from this inexorable questioning, from the humiliating accusation that

144

she was a batty sensation-seeker driven mad by the meno-pause.

Pamir then made her tell her story again. If I had any-thing to hide, it would certainly have come out during this remorseless questioning, thought Agatha.

At last she was free to go. The others, apart from Charles, had disappeared.

"You look awful," said Charles. "Rough time?"

"It was grim, He accused me of the murders."

"Why?"

"He thinks I am a sensation-seeker driven potty by the menopause, and not having any murders here to investigate, decided to manufacture some of my own."

Charles's eyes crinkled up with laughter. "That's funny."

"It's not funny at all," said Agatha furiously.

A secretary came out and told them a car was ready to take them home. They travelled in silence, Agatha thinking that she really must find out who murdered Rose and Harry or she would be damned forever as a madwoman.

At the villa, where the press were fortunately absent, Agatha said she would like to lie down and read.

She tried to concentrate on a novel about the complexi-ties of broken marriages, but finally felt too restless to go on reading.

When she emerged from her room, it was to find that Charles had gone off somewhere. Not wanting to be on her own in the villa, she took her own rented car and drove into Kyrenia and parked behind the post office. She walked down the main street looking at the shops, and then saw the turning to the left where she had first pursued James and met Bilal. She turned along the street, wondering suddenly if Bilal was working at his dry-cleaning and laundry business.

He left his work when he saw her hovering in the door-way. "Mrs. Raisin!" he cried. "I was just trying to call you. How are you?"

"Shattered," said Agatha.

"It is the terrible business," said Bilal. "Coffee?"

"Yes, please."

He placed two chairs and a wooden box to act as a table outside his shop and went to the café next door and came back with a tray on which were two cups of Turkish coffee and two glasses of water.

"The owners have been phoning me and Jackie from Australia," said Bilal. "They would like Mr. Lacey to call them."

"I meant to phone you about that. Mr. Lacey has gone to Turkey. If I'm still here after the month's rent has run out, I'll pay you for another month."

"Why has Mr. Lacey gone? I thought none of you was supposed to leave."

"He just took off," said Agatha. Her eyes suddenly filled with tears. Oh, James, how could you? Where are you?

Bilal handed her a clean handkerchief and looked at her sympathetically while she blew her nose, so sympathetically that Agatha found herself telling him everything.

"The police here are very good," said Bilal. "Just like British police, Mrs. Raisin."

"Agatha."

"Agatha, then, why don't you just take a holiday. I mean swim and see the sights and forget about trying to find out who did it. Your own life seems to be in danger. Just keep away from them all."

Agatha gave him a watery smile, warmed and comforted by his concern.

"I think I might just take your advice, Bilal."

"And come to our place one evening for dinner. Jackie's a good cook."

"Thank you. And now I really must go." They both rose.

"It will be all right. It may seem like a nightmare now, but it will be all right, you'll see."

Bilal smiled warmly at her, and moved by his friendship,

Agatha put her arms round him and hugged him and gave him a kiss on the cheek.

And then, as Agatha turned to walk away, she saw Jackie standing a little way away down the street, staring at her, and behind her stood Pamir.

And Agatha blushed, suddenly aware of how that affectionate embrace must look to Pamir, let alone Bilal's wife. She walked towards them.

"I was just talking to your husband," she said to Jackie.

"So I saw," said Jackie drily.

"Looking for me?" Agatha asked Pamir with what she felt was an awful, false guilty brightness.

"No, I was on my way to speak to your landlords. I will call on you later, perhaps."

Agatha trailed off. Pamir would be confirmed in his suspicions that she was some sort of sex-mad, peculiar female.

Her mind was just beginning to accept Bilal's advice as she walked up to The Grapevine, deciding to have a drink at the bar. The bar was empty, the lunch-time rush being over. Agatha realized she was hungry and ordered a chicken sandwich and a glass of wine and sat down at one of the tables.

And then Trevor came in. At first he did not see Agatha. He asked for a whisky in a hoarse voice and then, turning from the bar with his glass in his hand, he recognized her.

He walked forwards and demanded, "Are you following me?"

"How can I be following you when I was here first?" demanded Agatha.

Now that she had decided to forget about the case, she was dismayed when he sat down next to her. The tables were out in the restaurant garden among the flowers. Sun slanted down through the leaves of a jasmine bush, casting fluttering shadows over Trevor's pink, bloated face.

"This is a bad business," he said.

"Yes," said Agatha, wishing he would go away.

"I mean, why Harry?" he went on.

Agatha's good resolutions disappeared as she asked, "You tried to punch Harry, didn't you, because he called Rose a slut?"

"I don't remember," he said, shaking his head. "I drink so much, get these big blanks."

"Why would Harry call her a slut?"

Agatha held on to the table-top, prepared to flee if Trevor lost his temper, but all his usual truculence was absent.

"He probably felt for Olivia."

"Did Olivia think her husband was after Rose? I mean, was there any reason for her to think so?"

"Could've been. Rose liked to flirt a bit. That was all."

"How did you meet Rose?"

"I was with my wife at this road-house outside Cambridge—that's my first wife, Maggie. It was our wedding anniversary. Maggie and I had been married for twenty-five years. Got married when I was eighteen. Well, we was sort of Darby and Joan, set in our ways. Got one boy, left home to work abroad, just me and Maggie left. Good housekeeper. Very quiet. Bit fat. Grey hair. Never went out winter or summer without gloves on. We was in the dining-room, but there was this long bar running along the edge of it and Rose was sitting up on a bar-stool.

"I can 'member that evening as if it was yesterday. She was wearing a short dress and she had all those diamonds on.

" 'Look at all those rocks on that woman,' I says to Maggie. And Maggie says they're bound to be paste. Rose saw us looking at her and she asks the barman something. I had told the restaurant to give us a good table because it was our wedding anniversary and the barman must have known, for next thing is that Rose sends a bottle of champagne over to our table."

"When was this?" asked Agatha.

"Three years ago."

"I thought you'd been married a long time."

"To Maggie, not Rose. Anyway, Maggie was very flustered and flattered and asked her over. I'd never met anyone like Rose. She sort of sparkled. She seemed to have a lot of money and travelled a lot. She asked me what I did and I told her about the plumbing business. I bragged a bit and said I was making a fortune. Maggie kicked me under the table, but I didn't want to let the side down in front of a rich woman. Maggie went off to powder her nose and Rose hands me a card with her phone number, winks at me, and says, 'Why don't you call round and see me?'

"When Maggie came back towards the table, I seemed to see her for the first time, all dumpy and those damn gloves and she had thick specs that gave her a dopey look, and I thought, I've worked hard all my life, I deserve a bit of fun."

Trevor sighed. "I called her the very next day and we started an affair. I couldn't think of anything but Rose, couldn't see anything but Rose. So I asked Maggie for a divorce."

There was a long silence.

"How did Maggie take it?" asked Agatha gently.

"She never could sleep proper. Got pills from the doctor. Took the lot."

Agatha looked at him in horror. "She killed herself?"

He nodded. "My son, Wayne, he hasn't spoken to me since the funeral. He said Rose had changed me into a monster. But all I could feel was free at last. I'd spent too much trying to impress Rose and the business began to suffer. Rose found out about it before we came here. By that time she'd got Angus in tow. She liked money, did Rose. I was terrified she'd leave me. And now she's gone."

His pink face crumpled and fat tears ran down his cheeks.

He took out a scrubby handkerchief and dried his cheeks. "It's like living in a nightmare. Rose was awful. She liked manipulating people. She liked her bit of power. But I just don't know how to go on without her."

Agatha made soothing noises. She wondered whether to

offer to buy him another drink but then decided more alcohol might make him truculent.

"How did your friendship with Olivia and George start up?" she asked.

"That was Rose. Before we went for that swim off the yacht, she muttered to me, 'Snobby lot, but I'll soon sort them out.' "

"Could she have met any of them before?"

"Apart from Angus, no."

"Is . . . is Angus, I mean, was Angus in love with her?"

"Angus was safe. He adored Rose and he respected our marriage. I didn't mind Angus." He looked around bleakly. "I've got to go." He got up abruptly and strode out of the restaurant.

Agatha finished her half-eaten sandwich and asked for another glass of wine, thinking over what Trevor had told her. She suddenly wished James were with her, so that she could discuss it with him.

At last she left and walked down to the car-park. The sun was setting and the mournful call to prayer rang out from a minaret. She got into her car and sat for a moment.

She did not want to return to the villa, to Charles. Charles had been kind and she was glad of his company, but she blamed her night with him for having prompted James to leave.

She drove west out of Kyrenia, but passed the road which led to the villa and continued on through Lapta and then ever westwards and up a winding road into the mountains, driving steadily, not knowing where she was going, only knowing she was reluctant to return to the villa.

She reached the village of Sadrazamkoy. She was down from the mountains now, and beyond the village the road degenerated, becoming broken and in need of repair as it wound through flat, scrubby country. She drove on until she found herself at Cape Kormakiti, or decided that was where she was after switching on the car light and consulting her guidebook.

She climbed out of the car and walked towards the rocks. A navigation light shone on a rusty gantry. The waves crashing over the rocks caused the rock to emit a weird clanging sound, like the tolling of the passing bell for the dead at the church in Carsely, thought Agatha with a shiver.

Then she realized her real need to get away from everyone came from simple fear. Someone was trying to kill her and she was terrified.

And even with James gone and her life in a mess, she felt that she had so much to lose: her home, her cats, her friends in the village. She could not regret the driving hard-bitten years building up a successful public-relations firm, for she was now comfortably off.

The very fact that she had admitted to herself that she was frightened made the fear begin to ebb. She turned back to her rented car. They would all know the number plate now and be able to recognize it. It might be an idea to swap it for another.

She drove back over the mountains and east to Kyrenia, again without stopping at the villa. Mehmet at Atlantic Cars was just closing up his small office when she arrived.

"I would like to change the car," said Agatha.

"What's up with the one you've got?"

Agatha looked at him thoughtfully. She did not want to go into a long explanation about how someone was trying to murder her and so she wanted another car that would not be immediately recognizable as the one she drove.

"Ashtray full?" she suggested.

He grinned and shrugged, as if inured to the vagaries and whims of tourists. He selected a car key, changed the paperwork and led her to a car across the road.

Feeling more positive than she had felt all day, Agatha drove back to the villa at last.

To her surprise, there was no sign of Charles, nor did he seem to have left a note.

She made herself coffee and a sandwich, not feeling very

hungry. She then went upstairs, undressed and went to bed. She began to read but could not really concentrate.

She found herself missing Charles and reluctantly remembering his love-making, what she could remember. It had been warm and pleasant. It was a pity she was so much older than he.

At last, she switched out the light after looking at the clock. Midnight. Where was Charles? She turned on her side and fell asleep.

Agatha awoke with a start as she heard the door opening downstairs. She was about to call out, "Charles!" when she heard the sound of a female giggle and Charles's voice, saying, "Shhh! You'll awaken Aggie."

"Who's Aggie?" whispered the other voice.

"My aunt," said Charles.

Agatha lay as stiff as a board. She heard them both come up the stairs, giggling and whispering. Then they went into Charles's room. More whispering, more giggling and then the unmistakable sounds of love-making.

Agatha put the pillow over her head to try to block out the sounds.

In the morning, Agatha awoke and dressed in shorts and a T-shirt and went reluctantly downstairs. She had no right to complain about Charles's making love to anyone else, and yet it was the very fact he had described her as his aunt which had hurt so dreadfully, had made her feel old.

Charles was sitting at a table in the garden, as smooth and tailored as ever.

He hailed her with a cheery greeting of "Where did you get to yesterday?"

"Here and there," said Agatha, sitting down. "Where is she?"

"Who?"

"The woman you bedded last night."

"Oh, her. Long gone."

"Who was she?"

"I went out round the clubs and pubs to look for you and picked her up. English tourist. Emily. Very nice."

"Will you be seeing her again?"

"Shouldn't think so. She gets her plane home today."

"Easy come, easy go, as far as you're concerned, Charles."

"Want some coffee, Aggie?"

"Yes, please."

Agatha sat under the orange tree and stared out to sea. It was a clear day and the Turkish mainland was a thin line on the horizon. She felt diminished. She had begun to think she had meant more than an easy lay to Charles, but obviously not.

He came back with the coffee and put it down in front of her. "Why so grim, Aggie?"

"I heard myself being described last night as your aunt."

"Had to. If she was going to actually meet you, I would have had to say you were my sister. You're too glam to be an aunt."

"You're soft-soaping me."

"A little bit. Cheer up. Where did you go?"

Agatha told him about her conversation with Trevor.

"Still think he did it?" asked Charles.

"I wouldn't like to think so now, funnily enough. It was an awful story. Poor Maggie. It was those gloves he mentioned. I kept thinking about his first wife and her whole nice, orderly life being shattered."

"People think high tragedy belongs to the Greeks and Shakespeare, but mark my words, Aggie, it's alive and well in the suburbs of England."

"I still think he did it," said Agatha, "and I think he's on the point of cracking up and confessing."

"And you want to be the one to whom he confesses?"

"Not any more, Charles. I'm sick of the whole thing."

"Good girl. Let's go to The Dome for a swim in the pool

and have lunch. Let's not bother speaking to any of them any more."

"What about the press?" asked Agatha.

"We can't let the press run our lives. 'No comment' and a smile will get rid of them. Cheer up. I have a feeling it will soon all be over."

SEVEN

†

IT seemed odd to be going for a swim, just as if nothing had happened, as if she and Charles were tourists like the other tourists. The day was warm and humid, just as the weather had been when Agatha first arrived.

At least she had now such a healthy tan that she had only bothered to put on a little lipstick. "Will the sea still be nice and warm?" she asked.

"Shouldn't think so," said Charles. "Not any more. But it will be refreshing."

They got their tickets for the pool at the hotel reception desk. When they emerged into the sunlight, the first thing Agatha saw was Olivia, George, Trevor and Angus sitting at a table in the bar.

"Ignore them," said Charles cheerfully.

But once they had changed, their path took them right along past the party. Charles went straight by without a glance, but Agatha gave a weak smile and got bleak looks in return.

155

The water was almost cold, but once she was in, became pleasant. She swam around energetically, trying not to think of the others sitting in the bar. Charles called to her that he was going to swim in the sea instead. Agatha waved and said she would keep to the pool.

Then, as she emerged up the steps, it was to find George Debenham. He appeared to be waiting for her.

"What do you think of this latest business?" asked George.

Agatha sat down next to him. "I'm so bewildered and scared I don't want to think about it."

"I wish we were all out of here and back home," said George. "There's a maniac on the loose."

"Do you think it's one of us, or some local madman?" asked Agatha.

"It must be some local madman," said George. "It can't be one of us."

"Trevor has quite a temper," volunteered Agatha.

"Yes, but he's understandably broken up about the death of his wife. I think someone's out to get rid of us all."

"I gather from Trevor that his son, Wayne, is very bitter about Trevor divorcing Wayne's mother, who committed suicide," said Agatha. "He's one with a good reason to hate Rose."

"I'm sure the police have thought of that."

"If Trevor told them," pointed out Agatha. She hesitated and then said cautiously, "I was surprised when you and your wife befriended Rose and her party. Not your sort, I would have thought. You made that pretty plain on that yacht trip."

"Oh, you can't be stuck-up on holiday," he said vaguely. "It seemed like fun at the time to get together. And then, after it happened, we couldn't really abandon Trevor and Angus."

"Have you and Olivia been married a long time?" asked Agatha.

"Years and years."

"How did you first meet?"

"It was at a party in London. I was in my early twenties. I had just finished university and Olivia was training as a nurse. We hit it off right away."

"And what about Harry?"

"Friend of the family, and a good friend, too."

"Wasn't it odd of Harry to suddenly want to go off to the beach? Did he seem worried about something?"

"No, in fact he was in good form, excited and happy. I pointed out our swimming-costumes were in the car, but he said he liked the sea and wanted a walk along the beach."

"Do you think he might have been going to meet someone?" asked Agatha.

"He only knew us. He hadn't talked to anyone else that I know about. We were always together."

Agatha hesitated and then said, "Didn't you ever get fed up with Harry always tagging along? I mean, this holiday. Wouldn't you rather Harry had stayed at home?"

"Harry was paying for this holiday. He was very generous."

That made Agatha think of George's debts. She itched to ask him if Rose had held out the promise of money, but decided not to.

"I suppose there's nothing we can do now," he went on impatiently, "but wait for the bone-headed police to decide to let us all go."

"I don't think they're bone-headed," said Agatha slowly. "I think Pamir is very thorough."

"He questions and questions without getting anywhere. I'm sick of questions. The hotel is at least keeping the press out. They're absent this morning because Pamir is giving a press conference in Nicosia."

Charles appeared and stood looking down at them with a quizzical expression on his face. "Join us for a drink," said George, looking up.

And that was a mystery, too, thought Agatha as they followed George to the bar Charles had grossly insulted them, she herself annoyed them, and yet they continued to be friendly, in the odd way they continued to be friendly to Trevor and Angus.

Olivia was not wearing a swimming-costume but a sundress. She was knitting a sweater, her fingers moving quickly. "I didn't bring any warm clothes," she said to Agatha. "I got some wool to make myself a sweater. We were wondering whether to go to the British High Commission and ask for help to get us all home."

"I think they'll want us to stay until the murders have been solved."

Olivia stopped knitting. For the first time she looked lost and miserable. "I don't think they'll ever find out who did it. We'll be here for years and years."

"They can't keep us much longer," said Charles.

Angus said, "Puir auld Harry. He was in better form yesterday than I have ever seen him."

"It's amazing you didn't spot him on the beach," said Charles.

"We were looking for someone walking along by the sea," explained George. "We weren't looking for anyone lying down with a newspaper over their face. I pointed out to Pamir it was a Turkish Cypriot newspaper, not an English one."

"And what did he say?" asked Agatha.

"That there are rubbish bins on the beach and one of us could have taken it out and covered Harry with it," said Olivia. "I'm getting burnt. I'm going to go up to my room to get some sun-cream. Come with me, Agatha. I feel the need for some female company."

"Wait till I change," said Agatha. "I won't be a minute."

When she emerged from the changing cubicle, Olivia was waiting for her. They walked together into the hotel. Tourists were checking in, tourists were checking out, all holidaymakers, all free from suspicion of murder, thought Agatha.

"I wish I were one of them," said Olivia as they walked to

the lift. "Someone with an ordinary life. Someone who's had a relaxed holiday and is going home without a care in the world."

When they reached Olivia's room, she found the sun-cream and went into the bathroom. "Help yourself to a drink," she called. "I won't be long."

"I don't want a drink," Agatha shouted back. "I've drunk enough on this so-called holiday to last me a lifetime."

At last Olivia emerged, her bony shoulders gleaming with cream. She sat down wearily. "Where's James?" she asked. "Any news?"

Agatha shook her head. "He's somewhere in Turkey. That's all I know."

"Poor you. Why did he go off like that? Was it because of Charles?"

"No, no. James has always been strange."

"Bit thick, leaving you alone to face the music."

Agatha thought it was a bit thick as well but she wasn't going to tell Olivia that.

"Your husband told me that Harry was paying for this holiday," said Agatha. "I hope being made to stay on isn't running you into debt. George must be worried sick."

Olivia looked at her in surprise. "Why should George be worried sick?"

"Because of all his losses on the stock exchange."

"What?" Olivia's eyes bulged with amazement. "How did you hear that?"

"Pamir told me," said Agatha, not wanting to betray how she had come by the information. "Didn't you know?"

"No, I let George handle all the money affairs. Always have. It can't be true."

"It seems to be. The police appear to have gone thoroughly into our backgrounds."

Olivia had gone very white. Agatha felt miserably sorry for her and wished she had not said anything.

"Did Harry know?" asked Olivia.

"I don't know," said Agatha. "Perhaps he might have left both of you something in his will."

"That's a terrible thing to say."

"Practical, though."

Olivia's eyes clouded over. "Was that the attraction of Rose? Money? George said she was really good fun and very bright and that I was being the most dreadful snob, but she was awful."

"Again, I don't know," said Agatha. "I wish I hadn't told you about your husband's losses."

"I'd need to know sooner or later. Oh, God, now Harry's dead, we'll need to pay this hotel bill." She clutched her hair. "I can't think!"

Agatha was feeling guilty. Olivia had enough to cope with without starting to worry about paying the hotel bill.

"Look," she said awkwardly, "if you're broke, I can help out a bit."

"That's good of you. But I'm sure the police have got it wrong. George would have said something."

When they returned to the pool, Agatha said to Charles urgently, "Let's go."

Fortunately he had changed out of his swimming-trunks. As they walked off, Charles asked, "What's the matter? You look as if the hound of hell is after you."

"I let slip about George's debts. Olivia knew nothing about it. She looked shattered. I wish to God I hadn't said anything. Harry was paying for their holiday. Now he's dead, they're going to be left with a hell of a hotel bill. I offered to help out."

"Why on earth? You barely know the woman. You don't like her."

"I was sorry for her," said Agatha gruffly. "She's not bad."

"You're a soft touch, Aggie. Where are you taking me for lunch?"

"I'm not that soft a touch. There's food back at the villa."

"Okay, you win. Lunch is on me. Here?"

"No," said Agatha, "the press will soon be back."

"I know," said Charles. "Let's get clear away. Let's go to Famagusta and find a restaurant."

Agatha agreed.

It was the beginning to a surprisingly pleasant day. They ate stuffed vine leaves and rice washed down with mineral water at a small hole-in-the-wall restaurant in the market at Famagusta, and then walked around looking at the shops and buying postcards.

They decided to stay on for dinner before making their way back along the long straight road and then over the mountains.

"Can't see the stars," said Charles as he negotiated the winding mountain road down into Kyrenia. "I think there's going to be a storm."

"No lightning flashes out to sea," commented Agatha.

"I feel it coming, none the less."

When Charles swung the wheel and turned the car into the road leading to the villa, they saw with dismay Pamir's black official car parked outside, behind a police jeep with a flashing blue light.

"What now?" groaned Agatha.

Charles parked and they got out. Pamir approached them. "Is that your rented car?" he asked Agatha sternly, pointing to where Agatha's car was parked farther down the road.

"Yes," said Agatha. "What's happened?"

"Shall we go inside?"

I can't stand much more of this, thought Agatha as Charles led the way.

They sat down in the kitchen under the harsh fluorescent light and faced Pamir.

"When did you change your car, Mrs. Raisin?"

"Last night. Why?"

"Why did you change it? What was up with it?"

"Nothing," said Agatha. "Someone has been trying to kill me, whatever you say, and I thought it might be an idea to change the car and get a different registration."

"For heaven's sake, man," snapped Charles. "Get to the point."

"The car Mrs. Raisin was renting has been found at the foot of an embankment off the Nicosia Road. The driver, a mainland Turk, was found dead at the wheel. He rented the car this morning. So I must ask you what you have both been doing today."

Wearily they went through their day but Agatha omitted out of a queer sort of loyalty to Olivia to tell Pamir about their conversation. She thought about hurt and lost Trevor and shocked and frightened Olivia and began to feel a queer bond with them.

After over an hour of questioning, Pamir rose and said, "We are having the car investigated. The driver stank of alcohol, so he might simply have gone off the road."

"Why didn't you say so in the first place?" yelled Agatha, suddenly furious. "You've been letting me think that someone thought I was still using that car and tampered with it, you who didn't believe anything about the attacks on me. I'm sick of this. I have nothing to do with all this, and neither has Charles. I just want to go home!"

"We'll see. Meanwhile, keep yourselves available for questioning."

Pamir left and Charles and Agatha stared at each other.

"Will this never end?" asked Agatha.

"Let's just go to bed and forget about it until tomorrow." He glanced at her out of the corner of his eyes. "You know, Aggie, I would never have picked up that Emily unless I was drunk. Don't know why I did that."

"I do," said Agatha. "You're amoral."

"Oh well, go to your lonely bed."

"That is exactly what I'm going to do after I wash the salt off."

Agatha had a leisurely bath, trying to think of pleasant things, trying not to think of absent James or of murder.

She fell asleep almost immediately.

When she awoke, she could hear thunder rumbling in the distance. So Charles had been right. A storm was coming. Her brain was tired out with worry, she thought as she cleaned her teeth. She hadn't a clue as to who had killed Rose and Harry, assuming that there was only one murderer. She had been lucky in previous cases, that was all. James had been right. All she had surely done in the past was blunder about—and blunder into the murderer and nearly get herself killed, which was just what was happening here, but without any result.

She would forgo investigation and try hard to keep away from Olivia and the rest and do something to make the days pass. Yesterday had been pleasant. The books she had brought to read were uninspiring. Perhaps she should take up knitting like Olivia, thought Agatha, having a sudden vivid picture of Olivia's knitting needles flashing in and out of the wool, those steel knitting needles flashing in the sunlight.

And then Agatha's slowly put down the toothbrush. Olivia had been a nurse. Rose and Harry had been murdered by some thin instrument. If not a kebab skewer, what about a knitting needle rammed home by someone who knew exactly where to place it?

Olivia! Olivia, who did not know about her husband's debts, and so was puzzled by the sudden strange attraction Rose had for her husband. Yet how could Olivia possibly not have known how deeply in debt they were? Surely besotted Harry at his age had made a will and, having no wife or family, had probably left all to Olivia.

Agatha's heart began to hammer against her ribs.

How could she prove it?

Just ask her, said a voice.

But I'm not going to make the mistakes of the past. I'll arrange to met her in the hotel lounge with other people about.

She picked up the extension in her room and phoned The Dome and asked to be put through to Mrs. Debenham.

When Olivia answered, Agatha said, "About what we were discussing, Olivia. I have a cheque here for you which might help. Please don't say no."

"That's very kind of you," said Olivia in a low voice. "George isn't here. We had a bit of a row about money. He's gone out for a walk."

"Meet me in the hotel bar," said Agatha. "I'll only be about fifteen minutes."

She went downstairs to tell Charles where she was going but found him gone. She wondered whether to leave a note for him, but decided she didn't have the time.

As she left the villa, the thunder rolled nearer and a fat drop of rain struck her cheek. By the time she reached the outskirts of Kyrenia, the rain was coming down in floods and she could barely see the road. She parked in an illegal parking place outside the hotel. Let the police fine her just this once.

She had forgotten about the press and looked nervously around the reception area but there was not a camera in sight.

She walked through to the bar, wishing she had a tape recorder. Even if Olivia confessed, what proof would there be?

But Agatha did not feel like turning back now. She felt that unless these murders were solved, she would be stuck in north Cyprus for months.

Olivia was not in the bar. Agatha ordered coffee for two. And waited. After ten minutes, when she was just about to phone Olivia's room, Olivia entered.

"Sit down," said Agatha, "and have some coffee." Agatha looked around. A couple were having coffee some distance away and the waiters were busy arranging cakes in the cold shelf.

"This is very kind of you, Agatha," said Olivia with such

164

sincerity that Agatha decided she must have made some dreadful mistake. A bright flash of lightning lit up the room and someone screamed outside in the corridor. Then a great clap of thunder seemed to rock the hotel to its foundations. Rain streamed down the plate-glass windows.

Weakly Agatha felt she should write out a cheque, hand it over and forget about the whole thing. But something made her say, "No knitting today, Olivia?"

"It's up in my room," said Olivia. "My knitting gets on George's nerves. He says I remind him of Madame Defarge."

And then Agatha found her courage. She would never forgive herself if she did not try.

She asked quietly, "It would be better to get it out, Olivia. You can't go on living like this."

Olivia stared at her, her coffee-cup half-way to her lips.

"What are you talking about, Agatha?"

"Those knitting needles, steel knitting needles, sharp steel knitting needles, Olivia. And you used to be a nurse. I think you had one in your handbag the night we went to the disco. I think you killed Rose."

"You've gone mad," said Olivia, putting down her cup with an angry click in its saucer and gathering up her handbag.

"I have not yet told my suspicions to the police. But I'll bet one of those needles has been sharpened and I bet you've still got it," said Agatha desperately.

Olivia slowly sat down. Another flash of lightning, another clap of thunder.

She stared at Agatha.

"Why?" asked Agatha. "Rose was a flirt, but apart from that time I saw them chatting on Turtle Beach, there was nothing really to make you jealous, was there?"

"You weren't with us that day we went to Othello's Tower," said Olivia wearily. She put her head in her hands. "Rose was everything I despised—vulgar, raucous, pushing. George laughed at all her awful remarks, but that wasn't all. When we were about to go to bed that night, George suddenly said he wanted to go out for a walk. I said I would go with him and he shouted he wanted to be alone.

"I waited a minute or so and then I followed him. He was walking quickly towards the harbour but he never turned round, so I was able to keep him in sight. He went right to the end past the fish restaurants and turned up that road which leads up to the town from the end. It was deserted, so I walked slowly, keeping to the shadows. The road curves round to the right, but there's a black patch of scrub off to the left. I heard them before I saw them. Rose was against the wall, her skirt hitched up and he was having her, my George. I felt sick."

"What did they say when you confronted them?" asked Agatha.

"I didn't. And I didn't say anything to George either when he returned. I was frightened he would leave me. You see, I lied to you. I knew all along about the financial mess we were in. You shocked me because Pamir said nothing to me and so I thought the police didn't know about the debts. I knew that slut had probably marked him down as her next husband to spite me. She was everything I had ever despised. What would our friends say? The shame would have been dreadful. I sharpened up that knitting needle and put it in my bag and waited for my chance. And that chance came at the disco. I felt nothing but a tremendous relief that she was gone."

"But didn't George guess anything?"

"Not a thing. I kept close to the others afterwards because I began to be terrified of being found out. And then you came poking around. I knew you were going to Saint Hilarion. I actually passed James, would you believe it? He was sitting with his eyes closed. When I didn't manage to get rid of you, I managed to hide on the hillside until the fuss died down."

"How did you get into my room that night?"

"I heard you book a room and picked the lock of the

166

maid's closet on our landing and took the passkey and re-placed it the next day. Why did you have to interfere?"

"And why Harry? Did he find out?"

"Stupid old Harry couldn't believe any wrong of me. But he got drunk and sentimental and said he had left me every-thing in his will. I saw how George and I could stick it out and return to our old life. At Salamis, I said to Harry if he met me on the beach, I would give him a kiss. The besotted old fool got so excited, I thought he might have a heart attack and save me the trouble, but he was there when I escaped from the others. I suggested we lie down like lovers on the sand. And then I stabbed him and put the newspaper over his face. No, the needle is not in my room. I buried it in the sand."

"But why didn't you just ask Harry for the money to bail you out? I'm sure he would have given it to you."

"George doesn't know that I learned a while ago about the mess we were in. George is a gentleman; he has his pride. He would be furious if I took money from a friend because he could not manage his affairs. You don't understand people like us, Agatha. We come from a different world."

"A world in which your husband screws Rose with one eye on her money? Some gentleman! Come on, Olivia. What on earth possessed a sensible woman like you to do such a dreadful thing?"

"You don't know what love is," jeered Olivia. "I've seen you running after James like some old dog looking for a pat from its master. I love George. Without him, my life would have been nothing. The Roses of this world are expendable."

"We'd better go to the police," said Agatha heavily. "I'll come with you."

"You'd like that, wouldn't you, dear? Your little moment of Girls' Own glory. 'Brave Agatha of the Upper Sixth solves the mystery when police were baffled.' But you're not go-ing to."

"You can't very well stick a knitting needle in me here," said Agatha. "People about."

"Do you think I'm going to leave my George with all the shame of being married to a murderess? You've no proof, and you never will have!"

Olivia rose suddenly and turned and ran out of the bar, leaving her handbag on the table. Taken aback for only a moment, Agatha recovered and then leaped to her feet and set off in pursuit. Olivia was heading for the pool area. Blinded by the rain, Agatha ran hard after her.

Olivia veered round the pool and jumped straight into the boiling sea.

"Olivia!" screamed Agatha.

She ran to the edge and crouched down, peering through the torrent of rain. Olivia's head appeared between two huge waves and then she struck out strongly, swimming away from the shore.

Agatha screamed and screamed, but the rolls of thunder drowned out her voice.

A watery shaft of sunlight shone briefly down through the black clouds and Agatha saw Olivia's head rise above a wave and then she disappeared.

Agatha turned and ran back to the hotel, shouting for help.

An hour later she was huddled in a blanket in the manager's office when Pamir came in. He stood for a moment looking down at her, and then said, "No sign of her. Again I ask you, Mrs. Raisin: Why did you not call us first?"

"Because I had no proof! I told you!"

"But now, because of you, we definitely have no proof, and we have only your word for it."

"You don't think she drowned herself for fun!"

"Again, we have only your word for it. You could have thrown her in."

"Oh, don't be so silly. The waiters saw her run out of the bar."

"She could have been running away from you. No proof, Mrs. Raisin."

Agatha suddenly sat up, her eyes gleaming. "I know. She said when she stabbed Harry she buried the knitting needle in the sand on the beach."

"Wait here," he said curtly and went out.

Charles came in fifteen minutes later. "I've been trying and trying to get to you, Aggie, but you seem to be suspect number one. What went on?"

So Agatha told him about her brainwave, about confronting Olivia and how Olivia had confessed to the murders and run off into the sea.

"Why didn't you wait for me?" asked Charles. "I was only round at the garage getting petrol."

"How was I to know that?" wailed Agatha. "For all I knew you might have been trawling north Cyprus looking for a female tourist to bed."

"Nasty. But I'll forgive you because you must be in shock. Pamir's swearing about there being no proof."

"She buried the knitting needle she used to kill Harry in the beach at Salamis. I hope they find it in this storm. And I hope her fingerprints are on it or they'll start saying I killed Harry and tried to pin the blame on Olivia."

Pamir came in again and Agatha looked up hopefully. "Find the knitting needle?"

"You are free to go."

"Why?" Agatha's eyes gleamed. "You've found something?"

"We had already searched their rooms several times when they were out," said Pamir, sitting down, "but we did not find anything."

"You didn't search me," said Agatha.

"Yes, your villa was searched when you were out."

"So what did you find to incriminate Olivia? You must have found something or you would not be letting me go."

"We found the knitting needle."

"A sharpened knitting needle. I knew it!" cried Agatha. But how did you find it? Where? Why? She only had to clean it and throw it away anywhere on the island."

"We are lucky she did not. It was one of my sharp-eyed policeman. We returned to search her hotel room for the last time. Believe me, we had taken everything apart. And then this policeman saw a little white knob of plaster in a stain on the ceiling. We knew about the stain. The man in the room above had let his bath over-run and it had soaked the ceiling. He scraped away the little bit of white plaster and dug into the ceiling. While the plaster was still damp, she had simply rammed the needle up into the ceiling. It had a sharpened point and went in easily. Then she had bought a little bit of plaster from a hardware shop and sealed up the hole."

Agatha gasped. "It was a wonder she didn't get it out and throw it into the sea."

"Not at all. She had no reason to. And digging out again after the damp plaster had hardened might have alerted us to its whereabouts, always assuming we were clever enough to guess that she had done it."

"You mean, I was clever enough to guess she had done it," said Agatha.

"How's George taking it?" asked Charles.

"He's a shattered man. He says if Rose were alive today, he murder her himself. Seems she lured him with a promise of bailing him out. He said he hated making love to her but he was desperate for money. Turns out he had asked Harry Templeton for money and Harry said he would only give it to Mrs. Debenham and George did not want Olivia to know. Harry said that instead he would take them on holiday. George said Rose promised she would give him the money when they got back to England. He said that Olivia had a complete nervous breakdown about three years ago. He hadn't told her about his debts in case that tipped her over the edge again."

"I must ask the all-important question," said Charles. "Are we really free to go?"

"You'll need to come to police headquarters and make a complete statement, Mrs. Raisin, and sign it. After that, you are free to go."

Agatha pulled the blanket closely around her still wet clothes. "Aren't you going to thank me for having solved the murders?" she asked.

"I am sure we would have got there, sooner or later," said Pamir. "In which case Mrs. Debenham would still be alive to stand trial. No, I am not grateful to you."

"Well, I'm going back to the villa for a hot bath," said Agatha. "I suppose that is all right?"

"Yes, just go!"

Agatha got into her car outside while Charles went off to collect his. She lit a cigarette. Above, the storm clouds were rolling away but a chilly breeze was blowing from the sea.

At the villa, she bathed and changed her clothes.

She had just arrived downstairs when the phone rang. "I'll get it," she called to Charles whom she could hear moving about the kitchen.

Wondering whether she was wise to answer it for it might be some reporter, she said cautiously, "Yes?"

"Agatha," came James's voice.

Agatha sat down in a chair by the phone. "James," she said weakly. "Where are you?"

"Turkey. Istanbul."

"Did you find any proof against Mustafa?"

"As it turned out, I didn't have to. By the time I caught up with him in Istanbul, he was dead, shot by the Turkish mafia."

"Why? I mean was he dealing in drugs?"

"He owed the Turkish mafia money for a drugs' consignment and the silly bugger gave them a cheque that bounced so they shot him. What's been happening?"

Agatha told him everything and ended up by saying, "How could you leave me in this mess, James?"

"I always think you are well able to take care of yourself, Agatha. Besides it seemed more important to catch someone who was ruining thousands of lives with drugs instead of one murderer."

"But you just left. You knew there had been two attacks on my life, and you just left."

His voice softened. "You're right, Agatha. I did behave badly. I'll be back in a couple of days and make my peace with the police."

"Oh, James," said Agatha, forgiving him.

Charles walked into the living room and called in his clear, carrying voice, "What about some lunch, darling, and then let's go to bed?"

Agatha flapped him angrily away, but the damage was done.

"Who was that?" asked James.

"Charles," said Agatha weakly.

"I am glad you are being well looked after," said James crisply. "You won't need me."

And he hung up.

EIGHT

†

AGATHA and Charles fought their way through the press outside police headquarters the following day.

She had been dreading meeting George, but this time, only she and Charles were in the waiting room.

Not Pamir, but another detective took down Agatha's statement. When she had finished, Agatha asked, "Has Mrs. Debenham's body been found yet?"

"Mrs. Debenham was found, yes, still alive, just. She must have been a very powerful swimmer. Attempts were made to resuscitate her but she died on the road to Nicosia hospital."

So she might not have been trying to drown but to escape, thought Agatha.

Agatha went outside and waited for Charles. He would have little to say. Simply that he had found her missing and had gone looking for her.

At last Charles came out. "Ready?"

"Ready," echoed Agatha. "Let's go to the airline office

and book our seats home. I've got an open return, what about you?"

"The same."

At the Turkish Cypriot Airline office near the Saray Hotel, they could not find anyone who could speak English and so were forced to go to a travel agent across the road.

"Tomorrow?" asked Charles.

But Agatha clung to hope. James had said two days. This was Monday.

"Saturday," she said firmly.

"Saturday!" exclaimed Charles. "Sorry, Aggie, but I'm going tomorrow."

"Suit yourself," said Agatha bleakly.

Charles hesitated. Then he booked a seat for the following day.

"I think you should come with me," he said, but Agatha was adamant. She had convinced herself that James would return.

Outside, great gusty clouds were blowing across the red roofs of Nicosia. They talked about the case on the journey back to the villa. Charles went off to begin packing.

Agatha realised that since James had left, the villa seemed to have accumulated a great deal of dust and the floor needed a wash.

She spent the rest of the day, cleaning energetically, stopping only for a sandwich and a cup of coffee, and at one stage to look in on Charles who was found in his room, fast asleep.

Agatha tried to fight down the miserable thought that James would not arrive after all, and that she would be better to go home on the same flight as Charles.

Then Charles emerged to suggest they should go out for dinner for the last time.

"There's an advertisement out on the road for a restaurant called Rita On The Rocks," said Charles. "Sounds intriguing."

They drove west along the coast through Lapta and found the restaurant on the far side. It was open-air with a swimming pool and full of the sound of British voices. Rita herself, an attractive middle-aged Englishwoman, was moving from table to table greeting friends.

"So they found Olivia," said Agatha bleakly. Charles gave her a nervous look. They had already talked and talked about Olivia, but Agatha kept returning to the subject as if she had not said anything about it before. He decided to humour her.

"Yes," he said. "Maybe she thought to swim to shore after the heat was off and emulate James by bribing someone to take her to the mainland."

"I suppose it was a miracle they found that knitting needle," said Agatha. "She could have got rid of it where it would never have been found."

"So you keep saying. You're not cracking up, are you? Forget the murder, forget Olivia. I'm going to talk to you like your father, Aggie."

"You're too young, Charles."

"Seriously. Give up chasing after James. Waste of time, waste of energy. You're only going to get hurt again."

"That's my business."

"This trip, you seem to have made your business my business, Aggie. Stop thinking that he really loves you. If he really loved you, he would not have gone off to Turkey for any reason and left you alone."

"He had begun to think I wasn't alone because of you," said Agatha.

"You see!" He pointed a fork at her. "You're already beginning to look for excuses for him and there aren't any."

"He said he would back in two days," said Agatha stubbornly.

"I give up. Well, we've had some adventures. One day I will look back on all this and scream."

A noisy group of British residents at the next table were

175

practising their Turkish, having started lessons in Turkish in Kyrenia.

Conversation between Charles and Agatha became difficult because of the noise. They decided to have coffee at home, asked for the bill which Charles handed to Agatha who paid it, and then they left.

Back at the villa, they drank coffee, and watched a Brother Cadfael mystery broadcast by the local TV station which was mercifully in English and then decided to go to bed. Agatha said if Charles left his rented car outside Atlantic Cars in the morning, she would drive him to the airport.

"Last night together, sweetheart?" asked Charles as they went up the stairs.

"No," said Agatha firmly, having visions of James arriving in the middle of the night to find them in bed together.

"Oh, well, I can't say you don't know what you're missing because you do."

"I'm too old for you, Charles."

"Didn't notice."

"Thank you for that, but see you in the morning."

Agatha slept uneasily. During the night, a car drew up on the road outside and she leapt from bed and ran down the stairs and jerked open the door. But it was only a late visitor leaving a neighbour's house.

She drove Charles to the airport in the early light of dawn. He turned before going through security and said, "I'll see you around, Aggie."

"No doubt," said Agatha.

"Aren't you going to kiss me goodbye?"

Agatha put her arms round him and kissed him. He turned away, and then turned back at the security gate.

"You're too good for him, Aggie," he said, and then he was gone.

With his going, hope sprang anew in Agatha's breast. James would come, and they would talk, and during the days that followed with no murders hanging over them, they would grow closer together.

For the next two days, she dressed in her prettiest clothes and with full make-up on, she waited, rushing out of the villa door every time she heard a car coming down the road.

By Thursday, she had decided that if she wore just a comfortable T-shirt and shorts and didn't bother about make-up, he would come. But Thursday came and went, then Friday.

She packed slowly, her heart heavy. She drove to Bilal's laundry and told him she would leave the keys at his home on the road to the airport if he gave her the address, but that James would no doubt be back soon.

"Will you ever come back?" asked Bilal.

"Yes, I probably will," said Agatha. "One day."

She said goodbye to him and drove back to the villa. The day was sunny but now there was a slight chill in the air.

Agatha tried not to think of James, tried to concentrate on neat packing. She felt she should go out for a last meal but could not bring herself to leave.

But all too soon it was the morning of her departure. She drove slowly to the airport, looking all the time eagerly at the faces of any drivers in approaching rented cars, still hoping to see James.

Even at the airport, she scanned the faces of the passengers, hoping by some miracle he had just arrived.

It was only when she had cleared passport control that she at last lost all hope of seeing him and knew if he came back to Carsely that nothing was ever going to be the same. She would never forgive him for having abandoned her.

The take-off was delayed for two hours because of some hijack crisis at Stansted. They got as far as Istanbul and then had to wait four hours in a gate which did not seem to have a tannoy system. From time to time, various officials would come in and shout at the passengers in Turkish and Agatha had to beg one of the passengers to translate for her. They were going to Heathrow, they were going to Gatwick, and then it was announced that they were in fact going to Stansted after all.

A charter plane took them off and Agatha slept and woke and slept and woke, seeing in her dreams Trevor's pink and angry face, seeing Olivia's head rising above the monstrous waves.

And then the last time she awoke, the plane was descending into bleak and rainy Essex.

She collected her car at the Long Stay car-park and headed home, home to Carsely, the ache at her heart lifting when she reached Chipping Norton and turned the car towards Moreton-in-Marsh.

Down the road into Carsely, wind and rain sent spirals of coloured leaves down onto the road in front of her.

As she turned into the lane where she lived, her eyes flew immediately to James's cottage, hoping to see smoke rising from the chimney, but it had a closed, dark, empty look.

When she walked into her cottage, her cats, Hodge and Boswell, uncoiled themselves and came to meet her. Her cleaner had said it would be better for the cats to be left in the familiar surroundings of home and she would come every day to feed them.

Agatha felt very lonely. She found she missed Charles. He had been such an undemanding and constant companion.

The doorbell rang and her first, stupid, thought was, "James!" And then she knew it could not possibly be James.

She opened the door and the vicar's wife, Mrs. Bloxby, stood there, carrying a casserole.

"The bush telegraph told me you had been sighted," said Mrs. Bloxby, "so I put some of my Irish stew in a casserole for you. You won't feel like cooking."

"Come in," said Agatha, gratefully. "I've had such an awful time."

The doorbell rang again. This time it was Miss Simms,

the unmarried mother who was secretary of the Carsely Ladies Society, balancing precariously on her heels and carrying a cake. "Welcome home," she said.

After that, Agatha's doorbell seemed to go every few minutes until her living room was full of villagers. She began to tell the story of her adventures to a rapt audience, but did not say that James had abandoned her, only that he had to go to Turkey on business.

It was late when they all left with the exception of Mrs. Bloxby. "What a home coming!" said Agatha, her face radiant. "It's so good to be back."

"There's one thing that puzzles me," said Mrs. Bloxby. "You said James went off on business. What business? I mean, you got to the point in your story where there had been two attempts on your life, and then you mention casually that James took off. I mean, wasn't he worried about you?"

So Agatha told the real story, about Charles, about James's bad temper and coldness.

"A most peculiar man," said Mrs. Bloxby. "At least this makes you free of him at last. What he did was unforgivable."

"You're right," said Agatha. "He's out of my mind at last."

And as the next few weeks passed, such seemed to be the case. Carsely enfolded Agatha and the whole north Cyprus adventure appeared like a bad dream.

The solving of the murders in Cyprus had appeared in the British press and on television but there was no mention of Agatha. "I am an unsung detective," she said to Bill Wong when he called round one day.

"That's us policemen for you," said Bill, his eyes crinkling up with amusement. "Take all the credit no matter what nationality."

"No murders for me, Bill?"

"Nothing. In fact, it's the quietest time we've had for a long spell and I like it that way. So what are your plans? I can't really believe you're going to settle down to a quiet retired life."

"That's all I want at the moment. Anyway, I've been doing detective work in the village."

"What!"

"I found where Miss Simms had put her reading glasses and I found the Fletchers' missing dog."

"Big time."

"Suits me. I've got the job of organising the village Christmas party for the old folks. That'll keep me busy."

"No men in your life, Agatha?"

"No," said Agatha curtly. "And it that's the way I like it. Who needs them anyway?"

"I'm beginning to think all women feel the same as you."

"Unhappy love life, Bill?"

"There was this girl who works in the chemists in Mircester. Pretty little thing. We had fun. She seemed quite keen on me. But she suddenly went off me and now she's being romanced by a tattooed ape from the garage on the Oxford road."

"Did you take her home to meet your parents?"

"As a matter of fact, I did," said Bill.

And that does it every time, thought Agatha, but did not like to point out to Bill that his formidable mother could probably see off any prospect, for Bill adored his parents.

The phone rang. Agatha picked up the receiver.

"Hullo, Aggie. Charles."

"How are you?" said Agatha who had begun to think that Charles had forgotten all about her.

"Bored. Let's go out for dinner."

"Who's paying?"

"I am."

"May as well," said Agatha ungraciously. "Where?"

"We'll go somewhere in Stratford. Meet you at Marks and Spencer in the centre."

"No, Charles, if you want to take me for dinner, you can pick me up here at eight."

"It's a long way round for me."

"I want to dine in Moreton," said Agatha firmly.

"Okay, Aggie, see you at eight."

"Who was that?" asked Bill.

"Sir Charles Fraith."

Bill smiled to himself. He thought Agatha had changed a lot. The old insecure Agatha would never have commanded a baronet to come and pick her up.

Agatha and Charles ate in a pub in Moreton and talked about the events in Cyprus. "I wonder how George and Angus and Trevor are getting on," said Agatha.

"I don't," said Charles, "In fact if I saw one of them, I'd run a mile. Any word from James?"

"No."

"So you waited and waited for your knight to come riding up on a white charger and all you were left with was the smell of horse manure?"

"You are quite amazingly insensitive, Charles."

"Yes, but I stayed to look after you and he didn't. Are you really going to have toffee pudding, Aggie? No fears about your waistline?"

"I'm tired of my waistline. I'm tired of exercise and strict diet. I'm going to kiss my waistline goodbye."

"Let me do it for you."

"Behave yourself and eat your pudding!"

Charles drove her back. More through habit than anything else, Agatha glanced at James's cottage and then let out a gasp. Lights were shining from the downstairs windows and smoke was rising from the chimney.

"James is home!" she cried.

"And so he is," said Charles, parking smoothly outside her cottage. "Why not ask me in for a night-cap, Aggie?"

"All right," said Agatha defiantly.

They both got out of the car. James came out of his cottage door and stood looking at them.

Agatha unlocked her door and said over her shoulder to Charles in a loud, clear voice, "Come along, darling."

"Coming my angel, my sweet," said Charles cheerfully.

The door slammed.

James Lacey stood there for a few moments and then he too went in and slammed the door, but with such force that the sound echoed along the quiet lanes of Carsely and set a farm dog up on the hills above the village yelping with alarm.

Turn the page for an excerpt from M. C. Beaton's next mystery featuring the feisty sleuth—*Agatha Raisin and the Wellspring of Death* . . .

ONE

†

AGATHA Raisin was bored and unhappy. Her neighbour, James Lacey, had returned at last to the cottage next door to her own in the Cotswold village of Carsely. She tried to tell herself that she was no longer in love with him and that his coldness towards her did not matter.

She had almost married him, but her husband, still then very much alive, had surfaced at the wedding ceremony, and James had never really forgiven her for her deception.

One spring evening when the village was ablaze with daffodils, forsythia, magnolia and crocus, Agatha trudged along to the vicarage to a meeting of the Carsely Ladies' Society, hoping to find some gossip to enliven the tedium of her days.

But such that there was did not interest her because it concerned a spring of water in the neighbouring village of Ancombe.

Agatha knew the spring. In the eighteenth century, a Miss Jakes had channelled the spring through the bottom of her garden, through a pipe in the garden wall, and into a fountain for the use of the public. The water gushed out through the mouth of a skull—a folly which had caused no end of criticism even in the grim days of the eighteenth century—then to a shallow basin sunk into the ground, over the lip of the basin and down through a grating and under the road. On the other side, it became a little stream which meandered through other gardens until it joined the river Ancombe.

Some lines of doggerel, penned by Miss Jakes, had been engraved above the skull. They read:

> Weary traveller, stop and stare
> At the water gushing here.
> We live our days in this Vale of Strife.
> Bend and drink deep of the Waters of Life.

Two hundred years ago, the water was held to have magical, restorative properties, but now only walkers paused to fill their flasks, and occasionally locals like Agatha brought along a bottle to fill up and take home to make tea, the water being softer than the stuff which came out of the tap.

Recently, the newly formed Ancombe Water Company had attempted to secure permission from the Ancombe Parish Council to drain water from the spring each day, paying a penny a gallon.

"Many are saying it is sacrilege," said Mrs. Bloxby, the vicar's wife. "But there was never anything religious about the spring."

"It is bringing a sour note of commercialism into our gentle rural life," protested a newcomer to the ladies' society, a Mrs. Darry, who had recently moved to the Cotswolds from London and had all the incomers' zeal for preserving village life.

"I say it won't bother anyone," said the secretary, Miss Simms, crossing her black-stockinged legs and showing with a flash of thigh that they were the hold-up variety. "I mean ter say, the truck for the water's going to come each day at dawn. After that, anyone can help themselves as usual."

Agatha stifled a yawn. As a retired businesswoman who had run her own successful public relations company, she thought it was a sound commercial idea.

She did not like Mrs. Darry, who had a face like a startled ferret, so she said, "The Cotswolds are highly commercialized already, bursting with bus tours and tea-shops and craft-shops."

The room then split up into three factions, those for the business plan, those against, and those like Agatha who were heartily bored with the whole thing.

Mrs. Bloxby took Agatha aside as she was leaving, her gentle face concerned.

"You are looking a bit down in the dumps, Agatha," she said. "Is it James?"

"No," lied Agatha defensively. "It's the time of year. It always gets me down."

" 'April is the cruellest month.' "

Agatha blinked rapidly. She suspected a literary quotation and she hated quotations, damning them as belonging to some arty-farty world.

"Just so," she grumped and made her way out into the sweet evening air.

A magnolia tree glistened waxily in the silence of the vicarage garden. Over in the churchyard daffodils, bleached white by moonlight, nestled up to old leaning tombstones.

I must buy a plot in the churchyard, thought Agatha. How comforting to rest one's last under that blanket of shaggy grass and flowers. She sighed. Life at that moment was just a bowl of withered fruit, with a stone in every one.

She had almost forgotten about the water company. But a week later Roy Silver phoned her. Roy had been her employee when she had run her own business and now worked for the company which had bought her out. He was in a high state of excitement.

"Listen to this, Aggie," he chirped. "That Ancombe Water Company—heard of it?"

"Yes."

"They're our new clients and as their office is in Mircester, the boss wondered if you would like to handle the account on a freelance basis."

Agatha looked steelily at the phone. Roy Silver was the one who had found her husband so that he had turned up just as she was about to get married to James.

"No," she said curtly and replaced the phone.

She sat looking at it for a few minutes and then, plucking up courage, picked up the receiver and dialled James's number.

He answered after the first ring. "James," said Agatha with an awful false brightness. "What about dinner tonight?"

"I am very sorry," he said crisply. "I am busy. And," he went on quickly, as if to forestall any further invitation, "I shall be busy for the next few weeks."

Agatha very gently replaced the receiver. Her stomach hurt. People always talked about hearts breaking but the pain was always right in the gut.

A blackbird sang happily somewhere in the garden, the sweetness of the song intensifying the pain inside Agatha.

She picked up the phone again and dialled the number of Mircester police headquarters and asked to speak to her friend, Detective Sergeant Bill Wong, and, having been told it was his day off, phoned him at home.

"Agatha," said Bill, pleased. "I'm not doing anything today. Why don't you come over?"

Agatha hesitated. She found Bill's parents rather grim. "I'm afraid it will just be me," went on Bill. "Ma and Pa have gone to Southend to see some relatives."

"I'll be over," said Agatha.

She drove off, eyes averted from James's cottage.

Bill was delighted to see her. He was in his twenties, with a round face and a figure newly trimmed down.

"You're looking fit, Bill," said Agatha. "New girl-friend?" Bill's love life could be assessed from his figure, which quickly became plump the minute there was no romance in the offing.

"Yes. Her name is Sharon. She's a typist at the station. Very pretty."

"Introduced her yet to your mother and father?"

"Not yet."

So he would be all right for a little, thought Agatha cynically. Bill adored his parents and could never understand why the minute he introduced one of his lady-loves to them, the romance was immediately over.

"I was just about to have lunch," said Bill.

"I'll take you somewhere. My treat," said Agatha quickly. Bill's cooking was as awful as that of his mother.

"All right. There's quite a good pub at the end of the road."

The pub, called the Jolly Red Cow, was a dismal place, dominated by a pool table where the unemployed, white-faced youth of Mircester passed their daylight hours.

Agatha ordered chicken salad. The lettuce was limp and the chicken stringy. Bill tucked into a greasy egg, sausage and chips with every appearance of enjoyment.

"So what's new, Bill? Anything exciting?"

"Nothing much. Things have been quite quiet, thank goodness. What about you? Seen much of James?"

Agatha's face went stiff. "No, I haven't seen much of him. That's over. I don't want to talk about it."

Bill said hurriedly, as if anxious to change the subject, "What's all this fuss about the new water company?"

"Oh, that. They were talking about it at the ladies' society last week. I can't get excited about it. I mean, I don't see what the fuss is about. They're coming at dawn each day to take off the water and for the rest of the day everything will be as normal."

"I've got a nasty feeling in my bones about this," said Bill, dousing his chips with ketchup. "Anything to do with the environment, and sooner or later some protest group is going to turn up, and sooner or later there's going to be violence."

"I shouldn't think so." Agatha poked disconsolately at a piece of chicken. "Ancombe's a pretty dead sort of place."

"You might be surprised. Even in dead-alive sort of places there can be a rumpus. There are militant groups who don't care about the environment at all. All they want is an excuse for a punch-up. I sometimes think they're in the majority. The people who really care about some feature of the environment are usually a small, dedicated group who set out on a peaceful protest, and before they know where they are, they find themselves joined by the militants, and often some of them can end up getting badly hurt."

"It doesn't interest me," said Agatha. "In fact, to be honest, nothing much interests me these days."

He looked at her in affectionate concern. "What you want is for me to produce a murder for you to investigate. Well, I'm not going to do it. You can't go around expecting people to be murdered just to provide you with a hobby."

"It's a bit rude calling it a hobby. What *is* this crap?" She pushed her plate angrily away.

"I think the food here is very good," said Bill defensively. "You're just being picky because you're unhappy."

"I'm slimming anyway. The wretched Roy Silver phoned me up wanting me to do public relations for this water company."

"There's a thing. Their office is right here in Mircester."

"I'm retired."

"And unhappy and miserable. Why don't you take it on?"

But Agatha was not going to tell him the real reason for her refusal. Days away at the office meant days away from James Lacey, who might miraculously soften towards her.

After they had parted, Bill went thoughtfully home. On impulse, he phoned James.

"How are things going?" asked James cheerfully. "I haven't seen you in ages."

"You've been abroad. I've just been having lunch with Agatha and realized I hadn't spoken to you for some time."

"Oh." And James's 'oh' was so frigid that Bill thought if he were holding some cartoon phone receiver there would be icicles forming down the wire. So he chatted idly about this and that while all the while he wanted to ask James why he did not give poor Agatha a break and take her out for dinner.

A week later Agatha had just finished her usual breakfast of four cigarettes and three strong cups of black coffee when the phone rang. "Let it be James," she pleaded to that anthropomorphic God with the long beard and shaggy hair with whom she often, in moments of stress, did deals. "Let it be James and I'll never smoke again."

But the God of Agatha's understanding owed more to mythology than anything else and so she was hardly surprised to find out it was Roy Silver on the other end of the line.

"Don't hang up," said Roy quickly. "Look, you've still got a grudge against me because I found your husband."

"And ruined my life," said Agatha bitterly.

"Well, he's dead now, isn't he? And if James doesn't want to marry you, that's hardly my fault."

Agatha hung up.

The doorbell went. Perhaps He had heard her prayer. She stubbed out her cigarette.

"Last one," she said loudly to the ceiling.

She opened the door.

Mrs. Darry stood there.

"I wondered if you would do me a favour, Mrs. Raisin."

"Come in," said Agatha bleakly. She led the way into the kitchen, sat down at the table, and gloomily lit a cigarette.

Mrs. Darry sat down. "I would be grateful if you refrained from smoking."

"Tough," said Agatha. "This is my house and my cigarette. What do you want?"

"Don't you know you are killing yourself?"

Agatha looked at her cigarette and then at Mrs. Darry.

191

"As long as I am killing myself, I am not killing you. Out with it. What do you want?"

"Water."

"There's water in the tap. Has yours been cut off?"

"No, you do not understand. My mother is coming to stay."

Agatha blinked. Mrs. Darry she judged to be in her late sixties.

"Mother is ninety-two," went on Mrs. Darry. "She is very partial to good tea. I do not have a car and I wondered whether you would get me a flask of water from the spring at Ancombe?"

"I did not intend to go to Ancombe," said Agatha, thinking how much she disliked this newcomer to the village. She was such an ugly woman. How odd that people could be so ugly, not particularly because of appearance, but because of the atmosphere of judgmental bad temper and discontent they carried around with them.

She was wearing one of those sleeveless quilted jackets, tightly buttoned up over a high-necked blouse. Her pointed nose, her pursed mouth and her sandy hair and her pale green hunting eyes made her look more than ever to Agatha like some vicious feral animal, always looking for the kill.

"Is there no one else you could ask?" Agatha considered offering Mrs. Darry coffee, and then decided against it.

"Everyone else is so busy," mourned Mrs. Darry. "I mean, it's not as if you have much to do."

"As a matter of fact I do," retorted Agatha, stung to the quick. "I am going to be handling the public relations for the new water company."

Mrs. Darry gathered up her handbag and gloves and got to her feet. "I am surprised at you, Mrs. Raisin. That you who live in this village should be aiding and abetting a company that is out to destroy our environment is beyond belief."

"Push off," said Agatha.

Left alone, she lit another cigarette. On and off during

192

that day, she turned the idea of representing the water company over in her mind. Of course, the offer might not still be open. If she was employed in the launch, then she would need to work very hard, and if she was working very hard, she would not be impelled to make any more silly phone calls to James and suffer the inevitable rejection.

A poor evening on television did little to lighten her mood. She ate a whole bar of chocolate and felt the waistline of her skirt tighten alarmingly. In vain did she tell herself that the constricting feeling at her middle was probably psychosomatic. She decided on impulse to take a flask and walk over to Ancombe and get some water for tea, and to take another look at the spring.

It was another beautiful evening. Bird cherry starred the hedgerows, orchards on either side of the road glimmered with apple blossom. She trudged along, a stocky figure, feeling diminished by the glory of the night.

The walk to Ancombe was several miles and by the time she approached the spring, she was weary and already regretting her decision not to take the car.

The spring was at the far end of the village, the unlit end, where the houses stopped and the countryside began again.

As she approached she could hear the tinkling sound of the water.

She was about to bend over the spring when she started back with a gasp of alarm and dropped her flask. For lying at her feet, staring up at the faint light from the moon and stars above, was a dead man.

Very dead, thought Agatha, feeling for his pulse and finding none.

She ran back to the nearest house, roused the occupants and phoned the police.

Waving aside offers of brandy or tea, Agatha returned resolutely to the spring and waited. Word quickly spread around the village and by the time the police arrived, there was a silent circle of people around the body. The skull above the spring glared maliciously at them from over the dead man's body.

Agatha learned from the hushed whispers that the body was that of a Mr. Robert Struthers, chairman of Ancombe Parish Council. Blood was seeping from the back of his head into the spring, blood, black in the night, swirling around the stone basin.

Sirens tore through the silence of the night. The police had arrived at last. Bill would not be among them. It was his day off.

But Agatha recognized Detective Inspector Wilkes.

She sat in one of the police cars and made a statement to a policewoman. She felt quite numb. She was told to wait and a police car would take her home.

At last she was dropped off at her own cottage. She hesitated on her doorstep, looking wistfully towards the cottage next door. Here was a splendid opportunity to talk to James. But the shock of finding the dead man had changed something in her. I'm worth better than that, thought Agatha, unlocked her door and went in.

She was just making herself a cup of coffee when the doorbell rang. This time she did not expect to see James standing on the doorstep and it was with genuine gratitude and relief that she welcomed the vicar's wife, Mrs. Bloxby.

"I heard the terrible news," said Mrs. Bloxby, pushing a strand of grey hair behind her ear. "I came along to spend the night with you. You won't want to be alone."

Agatha looked at her with affection, remembering nights before when Mrs. Bloxby had volunteered to keep her company. "I think I'll be all right," she said, "but I'd be grateful if you would stay for a bit."

Mr. Bloxby followed her into the kitchen and sat down. "Mrs. Darry phoned me with the news. If you look out, you'll see lights all over the village. They'll be talking about it all night."

"Tell me about this water business," said Agatha, handing her a mug of coffee. "I assume they were asked to make a decision on the water."

"Yes, indeed, and some very noisy debates they had on the subject, too."

"Who owns the water?"

"Well, it comes from Mrs. Toynbee's garden, but as the well is out on the road, that bit belongs to the parish. There are seven members of the parish council and they've all served for years."

"What about council elections?"

"Oh, those come and go but nobody else wanted the job and so nobody ever stands against them. The late Mr. Struthers was chairman, Mr. Andy Stiggs is vice chairman, and the rest—Miss Mary Owen, Mrs. Jane Cutler, Mr. Bill Allen, Mr. Fred Shaw, and Miss Angela Buckley. Mr. Struthers was a retired banker. Mr. Stiggs is a retired shop-keeper, Miss Mary Owen, independently wealthy. Mrs. Jane Cutler, also wealthy, is a widow, Mr. Bill Allen runs the garden centre, Mr. Fred Shaw is the local electrician and Miss Angela Buckley is a farmer's daughter."

"And who was for selling the water and who against?"

"As far as I remember, Mrs. Cutler, Fred Shaw and Angela Buckley were for it, and Mary Owen, Bill Allen and Andy Stiggs, against. The chairman had the casting vote and as far as I know he had not yet made up his mind."

"It could be that one of the fors or one of the againsts could have known which way he was going to vote and didn't like it," said Agatha, her bearlike eyes gleaming under the heavy fringe of her brown hair.

"I shouldn't really think so. They are all quite elderly, except Miss Buckley, who is in her forties. They have all led unblemished lives."

"But this seems to have stirred them all up."

"Yes," said Mrs. Bloxby reluctantly. "The debates have been hot and furious. And of course the villagers themselves are split into two camps. Mary Owen claims the villagers have not been consulted and she is holding a meeting in the village hall. I think it was due to take place next week but I am sure it will be put off in view of this murder."

"If it does turn out to be murder," said Agatha slowly. "I mean, he was old and he was lying face-up. He could have had a seizure, fallen backwards and struck his head on the basin."

"Let's hope that is the case. If not, the press will arrive and television crews will arrive and it is so beautiful here that we will have to suffer from more tourists than usual."

"I'm a bit of a tourist myself," said Agatha huffily. "I don't really belong here. It drives me mad when people in the village complain about those terrible tourists when they've just come back from a holiday abroad where they've been tourists themselves."

"That's not quite true," said the vicar's wife gently. "Carsely people do not like leaving Carsely."

"I don't care. They go into Evesham and Moreton to do their shopping, so they are taking up someone else's bit of space. The world is one planet full of tourists."

"Or displaced people. Think of Bosnia."

"Bugger Bosnia," said Agatha with all the venom of one who has been made to feel guilty. "Sorry," she mumbled. "I must be a bit upset."

"I am sure you are. I must have been a shocking experience."

And it had been, thought Agatha. Some women such as herself were cursed with the same machismo as men. Her first thought had been to say, "Oh, it was all right. I'm used to dead bodies, you know." But Agatha had been afraid of so many things during her life that she had gone through the world with her fists swinging until the gentle life of Carsely and the kindness of the villagers had got under the carapace she had created for herself.

"If it should be murder and I concentrate on that," said

Agatha slowly, "I might take this job of public relations officer for the Ancombe Water Company."

"Mrs. Darry said you already had it."

"What a gossip that frump is! I only told her because she called round to ask me to get her some water from the spring and said, more or less, that I had nothing else to do. She made me feel as if I were already on the scrap-heap."

"It could be dangerous for you if you asked too many questions."

"If it's murder, it will probably be quickly solved. One of the Fors didn't want Struthers to block it or one of the Againsts thought he was going to break up village life and pollute the environment."

"I don't think that can be the case. You don't know the parish council; I do. Certainly this issue has made them very heated, but they are stable, ordinary members of the community. Shall you and James be investigating it? You have both had a lot of success in the past."

"He has been very rude to me and snubbed me," said Agatha. "No, I shall not go near him."

When Mrs. Bloxby left, Agatha got ready for bed. The old cottage creaked as it usually did when it settled down for the night and various wildlife rustled in the thatch. But every little noise made her jump and she wished she had not pretended to be so brave and had asked the vicar's wife to stay the night. Then there was James, just next door, who must have heard of the murder by now. He should be here with her to protect and comfort her. A tear rolled down Agatha's nose and she fell into an uneasy sleep.

Another fine spring day did much to banish the horrors of the night before, and Bill Wong called, accompanied by a policewoman, to go over her statement.

James Lacey had seen the police car arrive, knew all about the murder and that it was Agatha who had found the body. He had assumed she would call him, for he was eager for details, but finally Bill Wong left and his phone did not ring.

Agatha phoned Roy Silver. "I've decided to take that freelance job with the water company," she said gruffly. Roy longed for the power to tell her to get lost, but the fact that his boss would look on the getting of Agatha as a great coup stopped him.

"Great," he said coldly. "I'll set up a meeting for you tomorrow with the directors."

"I suppose you've seen the papers," said Agatha.

"What about?"

"The chairman of Ancombe Parish Council was found dead last night—by me."

"Never! You're quite a little vulture, Aggie. They'll need you more than ever to counteract the bad publicity. Is it murder?"

"Could be, but he was very old and maybe just fell over and struck his head on the stone basin."

"Anyway, I'll get back to you, sweetie, and give you the time you're to see them."

"Who will I be dealing with?"

"Co-directors, Guy and Peter Freemont, brothers."

"What their pedigree?"

"City businessmen, wheeler-dealers, you know the kind."

"All right, let me know."

Agatha looked at the clock. Nearly lunchtime. She decided to go along to the Red Lion, the local pub, and see what gossip she could glean. Perhaps James might be there . . . forget it!

Agatha Raisin and the Wellspring of Death
Now available from St. Martin's Paperbacks!

CPSIA information can be obtained
at www.ICGtesting.com
Printed in the USA
LVOW08s0845110617
537714LV00001B/4/P